D0192177

my cousin, my gastroenterologist

also by Mark Leyner

I SMELL ESTHER WILLIAMS (1983)

MARK LEYNER

my cousin, my

gas'tro·
en'ter·
ol·o·gist

HARMONY BOOKS
NEW YORK

acknowledgments

Portions of this book were originally published in the following magazines and
    anthologies:

"I Was an Infinitely Hot and Dense Dot," *Harper's Magazine*, November 1988,
    and *Mississippi Review*, Vol. 16, Fall 1988.
"Overture," *Guest Editor*, #1, Winter 1984.
"Enter the Squirrel," *Fiction International*, Spring 1987.
"Ode to Autumn," *Between C and D*, Vol. 1, #4, Winter 1985, and *American
    Made*, Fiction Collective, 1986.
"In the Kingdom of Boredom, I Wear the Royal Sweatpants," *Esquire*, August 1989.
"Saliva of the Fittest," *Between C and D*, Vol. 4, #3, Fall 1988.
"Psychotechnologies of the Somber Workaholics," *Rolling Stock*, #9, 1985.
"The Serenity of Objects," *Rampike*, Spring 1989.
"Gone with the Mind," *Fiction International*, Fall 1988.
"Lines Composed After Inhaling Paint Thinner," *Blatant Artifice* (Hallwalls
    Anthology, Vol. II), 1986.

Published by Harmony Books, a division of Crown Publishers, Inc.,
201 East 50th Street, New York, New York 10022

HARMONY and colophon are trademarks of Crown Publishers, Inc.

Manufactured in the United States of America

Library of Congress Cataloging-in-Publication Data
Leyner, Mark.
    My cousin, my gastroenterologist / Mark Leyner.
        p.   cm.
    I. Title.
PS3562.E99M9   1990
813'.54—dc20   89-27979
                                                                CIP

Book design by Archie Ferguson

ISBN 0-517-57579-5
10 9 8 7 6 5 4 3

FIRST EDITION

to my wife, Arleen—

the Smüx de Lüx

...who else?

i was an infinitely hot and dense dot

was driving to Las Vegas to tell
my sister that I'd had Mother's
respirator unplugged. Four bald men in the convertible in front
of me were picking the scabs off their sunburnt heads and
flicking them onto the road. I had to swerve to avoid riding over
one of the oozy crusts of blood and going into an uncontrollable
skid. I maneuvered the best I could in my boxy Korean import
but my mind was elsewhere. I hadn't eaten for days. I was
famished. Suddenly as I reached the crest of a hill, emerging
from the fog, there was a bright neon sign flashing on and off
that read: FOIE GRAS AND HARICOTS VERTS NEXT EXIT. I
checked the guidebook and it said: *Excellent food, malevolent
ambience.* I'd been habitually abusing an illegal growth
hormone extracted from the pituitary glands of human corpses
and I felt as if I were drowning in excremental filthiness but
the prospect of having something good to eat cheered me up. I
asked the waitress about the soup du jour and she said that it
was primordial soup—which is ammonia and methane mixed

with ocean water in the presence of lightning. Oh I'll take a
tureen of that embryonic broth, I say, constraint giving way to
exuberance—but as soon as she vanishes my spirit immediately
sags because the ambience is so malevolent. The bouncers are
hassling some youngsters who want drinks—instead of simply
carding the kids, they give them radiocarbon tests, using traces
of carbon 14 to determine how old they are—and also there's a
young wise guy from Texas A&M at a table near mine who asks
for freshly ground Rolaids on his fettuccine and two waiters
viciously work him over with heavy bludgeon-sized pepper
mills, so I get right back into my car and narcissistically comb
my thick jet-black hair in the rearview mirror and I check the
guidebook. There's an inn nearby—it's called Little Bo Peep's—
its habitués are shepherds. And after a long day of herding,
shearing, panpipe playing, muse invoking, and conversing in
eclogues, it's Miller time, and Bo Peep's is packed with rustic
swains who've left their flocks and sunlit, idealized arcadia
behind for the more pungent charms of hard-core social
intercourse. Everyone's favorite waitress is Kikugoro. She wears
a pale-blue silk kimono and a brocade obi of gold and silver
chrysanthemums with a small fan tucked into its folds, her face
is painted and powdered to a porcelain white. A cowboy from
south of the border orders a "Biggu Makku." But Kikugoro
says, "This is not Makudonarudo." She takes a long cylinder
of gallium arsenide crystal and slices him a thin wafer which
she serves with soy sauce, wasabi, pickled ginger, and daikon.
"Conducts electrons ten times faster than silicon . . . taste good,
gaucho-*san,* you eat," she says, bowing.

My sister is the beautiful day. Oh beautiful day, my sister,
wipe my nose, swaddle me in fresh-smelling garments. I nurse
at the adamantine nipple of the beautiful day, I quaff the milk
of the beautiful day, and for the first time since 1956, I cheese
on the shoulder of the beautiful day. Oh beautiful day, wash me
in your lake of cloudless azure. I have overdosed on television,
I am unresponsive and cyanotic, revive me in your shower of
gelid light and walk me through your piazza which is made of
elegant slabs of time. Oh beautiful day, kiss me. Your mouth is

like Columbus Day. You are the menthol of autumn. My lungs
cannot quench their thirst for you. Resuscitate me—I will never
exhale your tonic gasses. Inflate me so that I may rise into the
sky and mourn the monotonous topography of my life. Oh
beautiful day, my sister, wipe my nose and adorn me in your
finery. Let us lunch alfresco. Your club sandwiches are made
of mulch and wind perfumed with newsprint. Your frilly
toothpicks are the deciduous trees of school days.

I was an infinitely hot and dense dot. So begins the
autobiography of a feral child who was raised by huge and lurid
puppets. An autobiography written wearing wrist weights. It
ends with these words: A car drives through a puddle of sperm,
sweat, and contraceptive jelly, splattering the great chopsocky
vigilante from Hong Kong. Inside, two acephalic sardines in
mustard sauce are asleep in the rank darkness of their tin
container. Suddenly, the swinging doors burst open and a
mesomorphic cyborg walks in and whips out a 35-lb. phallus
made of corrosion-resistant nickel-base alloy and he begins to
stroke it sullenly, his eyes half shut. It's got a metal-oxide
membrane for absolute submicron filtration of petrochemical
fluids. It can ejaculate herbicides, sulfuric acid, tar glue, you
name it. At the end of the bar, a woman whose album-length
poem about temporomandibular joint dysfunction (TMJ) had
won a Grammy for best spoken word recording is gently slowly
ritually rubbing copper hexafluoroacetylacetone into her clitoris
as she watches the hunk with the non-Euclidian features shoot a
glob of dehydrogenated ethylbenzene 3,900 miles towards the
Arctic archipelago, eventually raining down upon a fiord on
Baffin Bay. Outside, a basketball plunges from the sky, killing a
dog. At a county fair, a huge and hairy man in mud-caked blue
overalls, surrounded by a crowd of retarded teenagers, swings a
sledgehammer above his head with brawny keloidal arms and
then brings it down with all his brute force on a tofu-burger on
a flowery paper plate. A lizard licks the dew from the stamen of
a stunted crocus. Rivets and girders float above the telekinetic
construction workers. The testicular voice of Barry White
emanates from some occult source within the laundry room. As

I chugalug a glass of tap water milky with contaminants, I realize that my mind is being drained of its contents and refilled with the beliefs of the most mission-oriented, can-do feral child ever raised by huge and lurid puppets. I am the voice... the voice from beyond and the voice from within—can you hear me? Yes. I speak to you and you only—is that clear? Yes, master. To whom do I speak? To me and me only. Is "happy" the appropriate epithet for someone who experiences each moment as if he were being alternately flayed alive and tickled to death? No, master.

In addition to the growth hormone extracted from the glands of human corpses, I was using anabolic steroids, tissue regeneration compounds, granulocyte-macrophage colony-stimulating factor (GM-CSF)—a substance used to stimulate growth of certain vital blood cells in radiation victims—and a nasal spray of neuropeptides that accelerates the release of pituitary hormones and I was getting larger and larger and my food bills were becoming enormous. So I went on a TV game show in the hopes of raising cash. This was my question, for $250,000 in cash and prizes: If the Pacific Ocean were filled with gin, what would be, in terms of proportionate volume, the proper lake of vermouth necessary to achieve a dry martini? I said Lake Ontario—but the answer was the Caspian Sea which is called a sea but is a lake by definition. I had failed. I had humiliated my family and disgraced the kung fu masters of the Shaolin temple. I stared balefully out into the studio audience which was chanting something that sounded like "dork."
I'm in my car. I'm high on Sinutab. And I'm driving anywhere. The vector of my movement from a given point is isotropic—meaning that all possible directions are equally probable. I end up at a squalid little dive somewhere in Vegas maybe Reno maybe Tahoe. I don't know... but there she is. I can't tell if she's a human or a fifth-generation gynemorphic android and I don't care. I crack open an ampule of mating pheromone and let it waft across the bar, as I sip my drink, a methyl isocyanate on the rocks—methyl isocyanate is the substance which killed more than 2,000 people when it leaked in Bhopal, India, but thanks to

my weight training, aerobic workouts, and a low-fat fiber-rich diet, the stuff has no effect on me. Sure enough she strolls over and occupies the stool next to mine. After a few moments of silence, I make the first move: We're all larval psychotics and have been since the age of two, I say, spitting an ice cube back into my glass. She moves closer to me. At this range, the downy cilia-like hairs that trickle from her navel remind me of the fractal ferns produced by injecting dyed water into an aqueous polymer solution, and I tell her so. She looks into my eyes: You have the glibness, superficial charm, grandiosity, lack of guilt, shallow feelings, impulsiveness, and lack of realistic long-term plans that excite me right now, she says, moving even closer. We feed on the same prey species, I growl. My lips are now one angstrom unit from her lips, which is one ten-billionth of a meter. I begin to kiss her but she turns her head away. Don't good little boys who finish all their vegetables get dessert? I ask. I can't kiss you, we're monozygotic replicants—we share 100% of our genetic material. My head spins. You are the beautiful day, I exclaim, your breath is a zephyr of eucalyptus that does a pas de bourrée across the Sea of Galilee. Thanks, she says, but we can't go back to my house and make love because monozygotic incest is forbidden by the elders. What if I said I could change all that.... What if I said that I had a miniature shotgun that blasts gene fragments into the cells of living organisms, altering their genetic matrices so that a monozygotic replicant would no longer be a monozygotic replicant and she could then make love to a muscleman without transgressing the incest taboo, I say, opening my shirt and exposing the device which I had stuck in the waistband of my black jeans. How'd you get that thing? she gasps, ogling its thick fiber-reinforced plastic barrel and the Uzi-Biotech logo embossed on the magazine which held two cartridges of gelated recombinant DNA. I got it for Christmas.... Do you have any last words before I scramble your chromosomes, I say, taking aim. Yes, she says, you first. I put the barrel to my heart. These are my last words: When I emerged from my mother's uterus I was the size of a chicken bouillon cube and Father said to the obstetrician:

I realize that at this stage it's difficult to prognosticate his chances for a productive future, but if he's going to remain six-sided and 0.4 grams for the rest of his life, then euthanasia's our best bet. But Mother, who only milliseconds before was in the very throes of labor, had already slipped on her muumuu and espadrilles and was puffing on a Marlboro: No pimple-faced simp two months out of Guadalajara is going to dissolve this helpless little hexahedron in a mug of boiling water, she said, as a nurse managed with acrobatic desperation to slide a suture basin under the long ash of her cigarette which she'd consumed in one furiously deep drag. These are my last words: My fear of being bullied and humiliated stems from an incident that occurred many years ago in a diner. A 500-lb. man seated next to me at the counter was proving that one particular paper towel was more absorbent than another brand. His face was swollen and covered with patches of hectic red. He spilled my glass of chocolate milk on the counter and then sopped it up with one paper towel and then with the other. With each wipe of the counter the sweep of his huge dimpled arm became wider and wider until he was repeatedly smashing his flattened hand and the saturated towel into my chest. There was an interminable cadence to the blows I endured. And instead of assistance from other patrons at the counter, I received their derision, their sneering laughter. But now look at me! I am a terrible god. When I enter the forest the mightiest oaks blanch and tremble. All rustling, chirping, growling, and buzzing cease, purling brooks become still. This is all because of my tremendous muscularity . . . which is the result of the hours of hard work that I put in at the gym and the strict dietary regimen to which I adhere. When I enter the forest the birds become incontinent with fear so there's this torrential downpour of shit from the trees. And I stride through—my whistle is like an earsplitting fife being played by a lunatic with a bloody bandage around his head. And the sunlight, rent into an incoherence of blazing vectors, illuminates me: a shimmering, serrated monster!

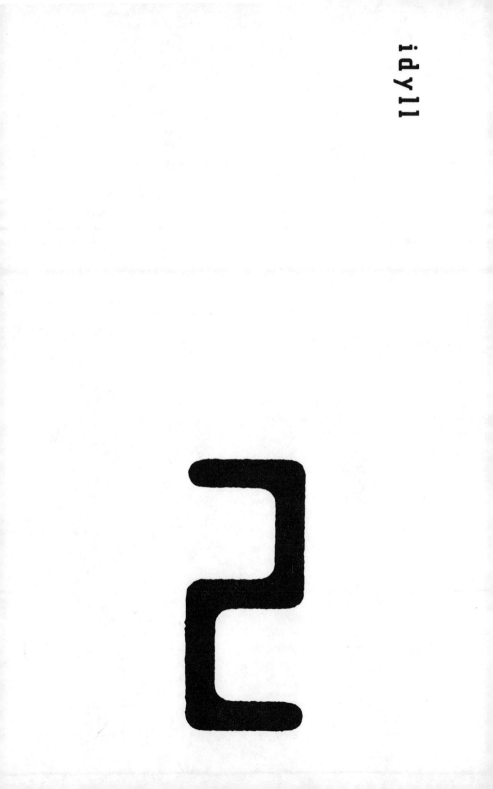

2

I was reading an article that contained the words "vineyards, orchards, and fields bountiful with fruits and vegetables; sheeps and goats graze on hillsides of lush greenery" and I realized that in five months none of these things would exist and I realized that as the last sheep on earth is skinned, boned, filleted, and flash-frozen, Arleen and I would probably be making love for the last time, mingling—for the last time—the sweet smell of her flesh which is like hyacinths and narcissus with the virile tang of my own which is like pond scum and headcheese and then I realized that the only thing that would distinguish me in the eyes of posterity from—for instance—those three sullen Chinese yuppies slumped over in their bentwood chairs at the most elegant McDonald's in the world is that I wrote the ads that go: "Suddenly There's Vancouver!"

fugitive from a centrifuge

Dad was in the basement centrifuging mouse spleen hybridoma, when I informed him that I'd enrolled at the Wilford Military Academy of Beauty.

The spirit, pride, and discipline I acquired during the rigors of the Academy would remain with me for the rest of my life. I'd never forget the Four Cardinal Principles: Teamwork; Positive Attitude; Hair That's Swinging and Bouncy, Not Plastered or Pinned Down; and Hair That's Clean, Shiny, and Well-Nourished. Years after I graduated, I'd occasionally rummage through the trunk in the attic and dust off the vinyl, flesh-colored pedicure training foot that was issued to each new beauty cadet. I'd give each toenail a fresh coat of polish, and the memories would come cascading back... memories of being unceremoniously roused in the middle of the night and sent off on 25-mile tactical missions with full pack which included poncho, mess kit, C rations, canteen, first-aid kit, compass, lean-to, entrenching tool, rinse, conditioner, setting lotion, two brushes (natural bristle and nylon), two sets of rollers (sponge and electric), barrettes, bobby pins, plastic-coated rubber bands, and a standard-issue 1,500-watt blow-dryer.

On our last mission—our "final exam"—we were airlifted to a remote region, and we parachuted directly into a hostile enclave. We had to subdue the enemy using hand-to-hand tactics like tae kwon do and pugil sticks, cut their hair in styles appropriate to their particular face shapes, and give them perms.

When we look back upon our childhoods, how terribly painful it can be. The people whom we loved seem to float across our hearts (like those entoptic specks that drift across our eyeballs), tantalizing us with the proximity of their impossibility.

When I graduated from the Wilford Military Academy of Beauty, my poor diabetic mother was sixty-one, blind, and obese. She'd sit out on the stoop hour after hour, plaintively plucking her untuned banjo. We never seemed to have much money even though Dad made about $60,000, which was an upper-echelon salary at that time—Dad was a senior partner at Chesek & Swenarton, one of the "Big 8" accounting firms. But he spent most of his money on his mistress. Although it disappointed me terribly that he wasn't able to spend more time with us at home—he usually spent Thanksgivings and Christmases and summer vacations with his girlfriend—I didn't resent his infidelity. Mom was extremely fat, she wore the same tattered tank top every day, her back and shoulders were covered with acne and boils, she wouldn't use the toilet. Dad, on the other hand, was quite handsome, athletic, vigorous, dapper—a cross between Errol Flynn and Sir Laurence Olivier. He'd come home after a long productive day at the office to find Mom in her soiled rocking chair on the stoop, endlessly strumming those atonal arpeggios on her banjo. But to me, to a boy, to her *son*, she was everything. She was wise . . . and she was clairvoyant. I'll never forget it—it was the summer of 1954—we were all at an Italian restaurant in Belmar, New Jersey, and Mom suddenly collapsed face first into a hot dish of eggplant parmigiana. And she lifted her head up, her face covered with steaming sauce and mozzarella cheese, and she predicted in an eerie, oracular monotone the establishment of the European Common Market in 1958, the seizure by North Korea of the U.S. Navy ship *Pueblo* in 1968, and the nation's first compulsory seat-belt law enacted in New York in 1984.

When Elvis Presley, in the song "Jailhouse Rock," sang the lyrics "If you can't find a partner, grab a wooden chair," he freed a generation of young people to love furniture and, by extension, to love any inanimate object in a way that heretofore would have been strictly verboten.

Soon psychopathology replaced ethnicity as the critical demographic determinant. There were no longer Italian neighborhoods, or Cuban neighborhoods, or Irish or Greek neighborhoods. There were Anorexic neighborhoods, and Narcissistic neighborhoods, and Manic and Compulsive neighborhoods. There was no longer a Columbus Day parade or a Puerto Rico Day parade; there was an Agoraphobics Day parade. Fifth Avenue lined with police barricades, traffic diverted. But, of course, the designated route was empty, utterly desolate, because the paraders, the spectators, even the Grand Marshal himself—agoraphobics each and every one—had all stayed away, each locked within the "safety" of his or her own home.

Corruption was epidemic, achieving its absolute apotheosis when the palsied 94-year-old godfather of the Mafia family which controlled organized crime in Louisiana was actually crowned Miss Universe in Taipei, Taiwan, and presented with a ruby ring, a tiara, a Renault, $8,000 in cash, and a year's worth of cosmetics from Avon.

On any given weekday morning, an astonishing procession of well-heeled mothers with Louis Vuitton bags slung across salon-browned shoulders could be seen escorting their children who were themselves resplendently outfitted in cute Oshkosh overalls or, better yet, pricey Laura Ashley kiddie casuals. The procession wended its way to the outskirts of the city, under a dilapidated trestle, past leaking barrels of sludge laden with

PCBs, where it wasn't unusual to see, among hordes of surfeited rats, the partially decomposed body of either a cult murder victim or the victim of a Colombian coke cartel assassination or simply a teenage derelict comatose atop a heap of empty Robitussin bottles. There you'd find the open-air "schoolroom" of the remarkable peripatetic teacher, Uchitel. Uchitel, who appeared to be in his late 40s, wore a caftan, loafers, and a baseball cap that said SURF'S UP. Beneath his wrap, his completely hairless body (he suffered from alopecia) smelled really good (patchouli). Who was this Uchitel? Why did he live and teach in toxic squalor? Why did these snotty, status-crazed, acquisitive mothers brave the dangerous urban outback and actually leave their precious pampered babies with this enigmatic vagrant? The legend began years ago when a wealthy woman reported her little seven-year-old son, Trevor, missing. After four days, police found him—unharmed—in the care of Uchitel, at the dismal chez-Uchitel. One week later, Trevor— who heretofore could barely concentrate long enough to comprehend a three-word sentence—was accepted into a postdoctoral high-energy physics program at Stanford. Fifteen days after his so-called abduction, Trevor was made Senior Space Policy Analyst at the Lawrence Livermore Laboratory.

It was through Uchitel that I met ... Olivia.

Olivia had just returned from the badlands of Patagonia, where she'd been excavating for dinosaur fossils, to accept a position as Dean of Admissions at the Uchitel School.

I had just been fired from McDonald's for refusing to wear a kilt during product launch week for their new McHaggis sandwich. (Haggis is the traditional Scottish dish that consists of the heart, liver, and lungs of a sheep minced with suet, onions, oatmeal, and seasonings and boiled in the stomach of the animal.)

When I first met Olivia, I was a bit stilted in the way I expressed myself. I'd say things like: "Would you care for a cookie and a glass of the fluid secretions of the bovine mammary gland?"

But Olivia taught me to be insouciant.

And soon after we met, we made a pact that if we were on a plane that was crashing, we'd grab the Walkman off someone's head, we'd grab three or four little bottles of Scotch, and we'd fuck—so that we'd die in our kind of glory—in that ecstatic maelstrom of booze and rock 'n' roll and orgasm. But remember that time when we ripped the Walkman off a Hasidic boy's head, plundered the cocktail cart and slugged down the booze, tore each other's clothes off, and then started going at it right in the aisle, and the stewardess came up to us and said: "It's only turbulence"?

We decided to take a trip to celebrate our first year together, and I asked Olivia where she'd especially like to go.

"I want to go to that asteroid where they breed the gladiator-drones," she said.

The asteroid of choice boasted a new luxury hotel and a miscellany of guest houses and bed and breakfast inns, and I asked Olivia where she'd especially like to stay.

"The new luxury hotel ... 125 floors of elegant design and sumptuous appointments rise within a sleek monolith of glass and steel, surrounded by a moat of pure mercury," she said, reading from the brochure.

Perhaps it was the extraordinarily mirthful outpouring of song from a wake-up chorus of XYY-chromosome gladiator-drones outside our door that first morning at the hotel that inspired me to reach across the bed and gently place my hand on the slightly convex belly of sleeping Olivia and then put my lips to hers—her breath still pungent with the previous night's escargot, snake and eggs, aduki beans *all'aglio,* and midnight snack of onion bagel with cream cheese, chives, and slivered scungilli—and kiss her with unbridled ardor. Or perhaps it was just because I was absolutely crazy about her.

That night we were standing on the balcony overlooking the mercury moat and the balcony collapsed and as we fell we were insouciant, we continued to nurse our Harvey Wallbangers and say things like: "You look simply radiant tonight."

When we returned from the asteroid, we purchased a home.

We had a rather large thing in our home and one day it got a hold of Bev and Jimmy's schnauzer. It was a buttocks-shaped seat-testing machine used by airlines. We examined the house with ultraviolet light because granulated schnauzer fluoresces; we scrutinized the carpet for the white glow of schnauzer.

Bev and Jimmy were from different cultures. Bev was from a pagan, matriarchal, moon-worshipping, earth-related stone culture and Jimmy was from a Christian, patriarchal, sun-worshipping, heaven-related bronze culture. But one thing upon which they completely agreed was suing Olivia and me for the freak pulverization of the schnauzer.

Luckily for us, Bev was distracted by another lawsuit she'd recently initiated. Bev was a speech pathologist. She had a twelve-year-old patient named Bob. Bob had been in school one day standing in front of his speech class giving an extemporaneous talk. The assignment he'd been given was to describe driving on Interstate 80 through the Midwest. Suddenly Bob couldn't speak properly. He had suffered some form of spontaneous aphasia. But it wasn't total aphasia. He could speak, but only in a staccato telegraphic style. Here's how he described driving through the Midwest on Interstate 80: "Corn corn corn corn Stuckey's. Corn corn corn corn Stuckey's." His parents took him to a hospital and they performed a CAT scan and an MRI scan and a PET scan and digital subtraction angiography and they found nothing wrong. So they took him to see a speech pathologist. Bev. One day, Bob was in session with Bev when a waterbug crawled out into the middle of the floor and signaled somehow to Bob. Whether it used its legs to communicate via sign language or exuded some sort of pheromone, no one knows. But Bob was cured. He began to speak in full sentences, saying things like: "Oh yes, with respect to the Interstate ... Whereas prostitution constitutes the commoditization of desire, the tollbooth exchange constitutes the eroticization of commoditized mobility—the tactile exchange of coins, a tryst in the night on the highway, albeit a surveillance, a regulation," etc. etc. Bev was charmed by the waterbug and decided to keep him as a pet. One day, Bev discovered a lump on the waterbug's thorax. She took him in to see the top entomological dermatologist in Kansas City who said that it was a benign tumor. He said he'd burn it off right there in the office using a magnifying glass and sunlight. But while he was performing the procedure, something distracted him and he momentarily lost control of the magnified sunbeam and the bug was incinerated. Bev sued for malpractice.

Our lawyer convinced Bev and Jimmy to drop the schnauzer-pulverization litigation and devote themselves completely to the waterbug-incineration malpractice case. Our lawyer's name was Knobloch. Harvard Law. Class of '64.

Introducing Gary P. Knobloch, attorney at law. I first hired Gary to aid in the administration of my mother's estate and the distribution of its assets which included the DeFrancesco Diamond—a 63.19-carat gem worth $1.5 million—that my mother had bequeathed to me. Gary lived in a sweltering vermin-infested apartment. I couldn't figure out why. The guy put over $180,000 in his pocket every year. So why the disgusting pad? I'd find out.

In appreciation of his efforts in settling the Bev and Jimmy matter, I gave him an old Radio Shack brand air conditioner/personal computer. Four megabytes of RAM, 256 kilobytes of ROM, and about 1,600 BTUs. You put it in the window and it cooled a good-sized room and did spread sheets and word processing.

About a week later, in the middle of the night, he called me up and told me to meet him in the parking lot of the old garter belt factory. And he told me to bring the diamond. The DeFrancesco Diamond.

When I got there, he wasn't alone. He had "friends." And he wanted the diamond. He wanted the DeFrancesco Diamond.

"How much money do you think I spend on prostitutes and cocaine every week?" he asked me.

"I have no idea, Gary."

"Guess."

"I couldn't even guess."

"Guess how much!"

"I have absolutely no idea."

They beat me. These were ruthless kung fu Chivas-sipping Hong Kong triad thugs in tailor-made silk suits and gold Rolex watches. I spit out a tooth and a hunk of bloody pulp.

"All right. All right. I'll guess. $6,000 a week."

Gary appeared crestfallen.

"No," he said, "it's only $4,500."

"Gary, that's exactly why I didn't want to guess. I'd make some wild guess and it would be higher than the actual figure so that when you told me the real amount you spend on prostitutes and cocaine every week it would seem diminished and anticlimactic compared to the higher guess and you'd be disappointed and embarrassed...it's precisely precisely why I didn't want to guess."

I put my arm around his shoulder. His goons started toward me again, but he waved them off.

"C'mon, pal," I said, "why don't you just go home and get some sleep...OK? C'mon...I got something for you."

I opened the trunk of my car and gave him a surge protector for his air conditioner.

As time passed, I became obsessed with death, dismemberment, mutilation, and torture, and—more specifically—with death or serious injury as a result of violent crime, plane or auto crash. This obsession with violence was well-founded. The incidence of brutality and accidental trauma had reached a level that appalled even the most pessimistic Malthusians. According to the Bureau of Violent Crime Statistics, the chances of being killed in one's own bedroom by a member of one's own family on any given night were 3 in 5. The chances of having an arm or leg slashed off while using public transportation were now 7 in 10! The chances of the criminal absconding with the severed limb and hiding it somewhere so that surgeons couldn't reattach it were a chilling 4 in 7! And the chances of being sucked out of a passenger jet were now 2 in 3—according to *Forensic Free Fall*, an industry newsletter devoted exclusively to accidental in-flight deplanings.

The military government cracked down on the public at large, banning deviations from quotidian routine.

But as the following diary entry indicates, such irregularities persisted: "May 20. A young commodities trader in business suit and sneakers walked into a deli and purchased his daily V-8 juice which, customarily, he'd put in his briefcase and drink at the office later in the morning. But inexplicably, the man took the 24-oz. can of vegetable juice out of the brown paper bag and—as the deli owner and his wife looked on in horror—drank it down on the spot, draining the can's contents with what Antoinette Orbach, a career counselor who'd come in for her usual fried egg and Gorgonzola on a hard roll, described as 'a gurgling sound—a sound I don't think I'll ever forget.' The man then proceeded to purchase one 59-cent can of V-8 after another and, standing in front of the register, gulp each one down, until in the middle of the fifth can, he became ill and stumbled outside where he was shot and killed instantly by the single bullet of a police sniper. Meanwhile, across town, a severely retarded woman who was unable to speak, feed herself, or control her bodily functions—never mind play a musical instrument—sat down at her stepbrother's hammered dulcimer and suddenly played a flawless rendition of 'Ease on Down the Road' from *The Wiz*."

The diary entry continues: "I'm chain-chewing stick after stick of sugarless bubble gum. It's the hottest day of the year and I'm in my wrestling leotard and I can't find anyone to wrestle with. 'Two out of three falls,' I suggest to Kenny. 'Maybe towards the end of the week when it cools off a bit,' he demurs. 'How about you, Andrew?' Andrew's a clerk at a clothing store for stout men and hyperpituitary giants. 'Greco-Roman, WWF, any style you want.' 'No, I'm going to Fire Island to beat the heat and relax with my love interest, Jane.' I go to the Korean fruit and vegetable stand because I always see my pal Ivan there, Ivan the Realtor. There's Ivan. His short-sleeved button-down shirt is sopping wet with perspiration, his breathing is labored, his eyes unfocused—he's clearly having difficulty coping with the 100-plus degrees. 'Hey, Ivan!' I slap him on the back—sweat flies everywhere. 'Hey, watch it,' snaps a Korean guy. 'You knocked that guy's sweat into the nice salad bar.' 'Sorry,' I say. I usher wet Ivan out onto the sidewalk. 'Hey, Ivan, do you want to wrestle, I've got an extra wrestling leotard that would fit you.' 'No,' says Ivan, 'I've got to go finish a letter to my sister Gretel. I'm trying to describe to her how beautiful the sunlight is when it strikes a particular skyscraper in the late afternoon, but without using the words *beautiful, sunlight, skyscraper,* or *late afternoon.*' 'All right!' I say, throwing myself to the ground and pounding my fist on the gooey macadam. 'I give up...I give up!'"

The man whose songs helped unionize thousands of workers in colonic irrigation clinics across the country was named Folk Musician of the Year in London, England. My cousin and three other noted gastroenterologists were scheduled to attend the awards ceremony as representatives of the American Gastroenterological Association. My cousin had an extra ticket and he was kind enough to invite me to accompany him to London. "What's more," he said dramatically, "there will be an official visit with the royal family!"

"*The* royal family?" I asked. I was skeptical because I'd known *a* Royal family back home—Joel and Muriel Royal. He was in pharmaceutical sales, she hausfraued and substitute-taught on the side. They had three kids: Joaquin, Orville, and Joey D. Joey D. had a tumor on his pineal gland that caused him to sexually mature at the age of four and a half. His tricycle had a turbocharged V-8 engine with double overhead cams that did 0 to 60 in 7 seconds.

My cousin's invitation was particularly fortuitous because only days before, I'd received a wire from a prestigious jeweler in London who said that he had an ornate antique platinum setting that would be perfect for the DeFrancesco Diamond— would I be interested, next time I'm in Britain, in bringing the diamond to his home and discussing the setting? I wired him immediately after accepting my cousin's offer: YES, I'LL BE THERE. WHERE IS YOUR HOME? He wired me back immediately: YOU'LL FIND IT—I EAT MEXICAN FOOD WITH THE SHADES UP.

Hats off to the Omni International Hotel in London! Their can-do attitude and their commitment to catering to the needs of their guests exceed anything that I've encountered in over 30 years of extensive business travel.

By way of background, about six months before I accompanied my cousin to London, I was privileged to have been invited to accompany a team of deep-sea researchers and Mitsubishi top management representatives on the maiden outing of the *Shinkai 6500,* the world's deepest-diving research submarine. I'll never forget my embarrassment upon arriving at the Mitsubishi Heavy Industries shipyard in Kobe, Japan. There I was in full deep-sea diving regalia, straining under the weight of $10,000 worth of state-of-the-art equipment. I heard a sharp knock on my diving helmet, turned on the heels of my flippers, and there was Takeo Yoshikawa, Director of Benthonic Research at Mitsubishi, grinning broadly, casually attired in pale-blue polo shirt, safari shorts, and espadrilles.

"My good friend," he laughed, "you look like an extra from a Japanese monster movie. *Shinkai* environment enables us to dress very comfortably—let's find you some suitable garments."

Takeo and his assistant, Yukio Yamamoto, found it hysterically funny that I'd actually taken a taxicab dressed in deep-sea diving gear. In fact, I thought I heard Yamamoto mutter the phrase "deficit-generating American, your protectionistic tariffs and economic jingoism will never obscure the fact that archaic management techniques and shoddy workmanship have caused American consumers to eschew their own country's products in favor of our own" under his breath, but in deference to my long friendship with Takeo and the importance of the *Shinkai* project, I refrained from pursuing the issue. I offered to go back to the hotel and change clothes, but Takeo pointed out that the *Shinkai* was scheduled for an 11:30 A.M. launch, leaving me no time to make the 90-minute round trip.

"We'll find a shop close by," Takeo suggested, and Yamamoto nodded, the trace of his smirk still lingering about his lips, or so it seemed. (In retrospect, it's more than possible that I'd projected my chagrin at being inappropriately dressed onto Yamamoto, perceiving hostile gibes and contempt where none existed.)

Finding a haberdashery near the Mitsubishi Heavy Industries shipyard was no easy task, notwithstanding Takeo's optimism, but we succeeded, and soon we were aboard the *Shinkai* and heading for the black depths of the East Pacific Rise, two miles below the surface, where volcanic vents continuously shoot out black clouds of 660° F sulfurous water.

Well, to make a long story short, I fell in love with the Rimicaris exoculata. Rimicaris exoculata is a species of deep-sea shrimp which inhabit the high-temperature sulfide chimneys at East Pacific Rise hydrothermal fields, feeding on the sulfur-metabolizing microorganisms that find the sulfide chimneys congenial. Using a sophisticated robotic specimen-collection arm, Takeo captured a dozen of these fascinating and exotic deep-sea shrimp for me to take back to the States and keep as pets.

Needless to say, the shrimp and I became inseparable, and, of course, I intended to bring them along with me when I accompanied my cousin to London. The problem was that during my stay I'd need a continuous supply of sulfur-laden 660° F water to provide an appropriate environment for the bacteria which my shrimp feed on. I wired the hotel, explaining my unique requirements. They wired back immediately: PLEASE BE ASSURED THAT WE WILL DO EVERYTHING POSSIBLE TO MAKE THIS A MOST PLEASANT STAY FOR YOU, YOUR DEEP-SEA SHRIMP, AND THE SULFUR-METABOLIZING MICROORGANISMS UPON WHICH THEY FEED.

Leave it to the zealous, resourceful folks at the Omni International. When I got to my suite and opened the door to the bathroom, I stood there, mouth agape, absolutely flabbergasted. In the beautiful sunken bathtub, there was a cold-water faucet, a hot-water faucet, and a specially constructed faucet that delivered 660° F sulfurous water. Kudos to staff and management!

My agenda in London was hectic, to say the least. In a single day, I was scheduled to meet with the jeweler about the setting for the DeFrancesco Diamond, attend the Folk Musician of the Year ceremonies with my cousin, my gastroenterologist, and then visit with the royal family. Finding the jeweler's home was no problem. Through the window of his villa, I could see him eating a tortilla.

I didn't expect the Queen's hand to be so sweaty, so soggy. I was also surprised that her accent was Southern and not British. I expected lockjawed noblesse oblige, but I got "Y'all come back and visit Buckingham Palace real soon, y'hear."

The day with all its glamour, pomp, and fanfare was exhilarating and exhausting. And when I returned to my suite at the Omni International that evening, I quickly doffed my tuxedo, slipped into my robe, had a Scotch and soda sent up, and stretched out across the plush chaise longue. Just then, the phone rang. It was Olivia.

"Does it sound like I did the wrong thing?" she asked.

"What?"

"Does it sound like I did the wrong thing?"

"Olivia, what do you mean?"

"Well, it had been an unusually long and rough day at work. There'd been a breakdown in our proofreading protocol and a mistake got through on an expensive pathogen identification wall chart—so instead of one of the panels reading 'E. Coli,' it read 'E. Cola,' and we'd already printed 10,000 pieces and the client wanted us to eat the costs and reprint the wall chart and my boss wanted the client to eat the costs and he insisted that I call the client and tell him that we wanted him to eat the costs since he'd signed off on the mechanical and the blueprint and never caught the mistake. It was a mess and it was unpleasant having to call the client and haggle over what was our mistake—it was really our lax editorial system that permitted the error to appear on the printed piece. Anyway, I got home at about 9 P.M. I popped a Lean Cuisine into the microwave and ate it in front of the TV. There was a miniseries on based on James Michener's *Lincoln*— the saga of the men and women who built the Lincoln Tunnel. It ended with the postscript 'In 1985, AM radio reception became a reality for Lincoln Tunnel commuters. It's a shame that Gordon Toltzis—tunnel-radio pioneer—couldn't have lived to hear his dream come true.' After I finished dinner, I felt exhausted and I decided to go to bed even though it was only about 10:30, so I went into the bedroom and I got undressed. And there I was standing in front of the full-length mirror, stark naked, looking at the liposuction scars on my thighs, when the phone rings. I picked it up and said hello but no one said hello in response. Then I started to hear some really peculiar sounds. It was as if someone had a Jell-O mold and he was 'spanking' it with a flyswatter, because there'd be this sort of muffled squishy slap and then a guttural voice moaning 'Sweet mother of God' and then the squishy slap and the 'Sweet mother of God,' etc. etc. I know I probably should have hung up but . . . Anyway, finally this guy started talking and he said he had a pizza for me, could I give him my address and he'd deliver it. And I told him that I hadn't ordered a pizza, but he said that I'd won it. I know I probably shouldn't have, but I told him OK and I gave him the address. In about a half hour this guy showed up and I looked at him through the peephole in the door and he didn't even have a pizza and I know I probably shouldn't have let him in—but I did. One of his eyes was sort of half closed, with a jagged scar across the lid as if he'd been knifed or something. After a while he asked me if I wanted to make love and I asked him if he had any venereal diseases and he said no, that he just had some symptoms. And I know that I shouldn't have, but I made love with him. Well, about a month later I found out I was pregnant. I realize that I probably should have gotten an abortion, but I decided to have the baby, and we got married. Then, a couple of weeks after I gave birth, he was arrested for assault with a deadly weapon, convicted, and sent to prison to do a 15-year stretch. I know . . . I know at that point I probably should have just filed for divorce . . . but I just didn't. So about a week before his birthday, I decided to go to the department store, buy him a gift, and drive up to the prison to give it to him. I was at that store for over three hours, trying to make up my mind between this really handsome gray turtleneck shirt and an ultrasonic humidifier on sale that I thought might be nice for his cell. I mean I just could not decide—I'd be standing on line at the checkout counter with one and then suddenly I'd be like: no way, he'll definitely like the other one better. And I'd bolt for the aisle and switch. And finally, finally—after three entire hours of vacillating between the turtleneck and the ultrasonic humidifier—I bought him the humidifier. So does it sound like I did the wrong thing? I know that he really likes turtlenecks and he likes 100% cotton, but the ultrasonic humidifier seemed so practical and I think $55 is such a great buy."

I calmly hung up the phone. My cocktail was evaporating to the ceiling, condensing, and drizzling back down into my highball glass.

I had dinner at a local Chinese restaurant. My fortune cookie read: *You will develop a pilonidal cyst.* So I tried to see Dr. Pons back at the hotel, but the nurse said: "Dr. Pons got a hernia taking off his cowboy boots." So I packed my bags and took a taxi to Heathrow Airport.

When Pan Am hired Jeffrey Bower as a pilot for its London to New York flights, it was apparently unaware of his lifelong obsession with the kamikazes—the suicide fliers of the "Divine Wind," the self-immolating archangels of the Rising Sun who steered their bomb-laden planes into the decks of U.S. aircraft carriers.

Approximately midway across the Atlantic, Bower suddenly banked our flight into a terrifyingly sharp 360° turn, the centrifugal force of which separated the passengers' red cells from their leukocytes and platelets from their blood plasma. He then took the jet into a suicide dive, aimed at the *QEII* which cruised innocently below. The effect on the passengers as the plane dove towards Bower's target on the water was traumatic. Many hyperventilated. Others showed agitated motor activity: complex twirling movements, writhing, flailing. Eventually the cabin was filled with sounds of gagging, retching, shrieking, exaggerated laughter, and choking. Many people were sweating profusely, some were in the fetal position.

I struggled out of my seat and made my way to the cockpit. Bower had drugged the copilot and flight engineer. Utter madness blazed in his eyes.

"Bower!" I shouted at him. "You're going to kill us all! Stop this insanity—I beg of you!"

Bower turned to me momentarily with a look of complete contempt before returning his attention to the trajectory of the jet towards the unsuspecting luxury cruise ship. (As I look back on the incident, perhaps, again, I was projecting my own very negative feelings onto Bower, but my sense of his contempt seemed quite genuine at the time.)

I realized that there was only one thing left to do if we were going to survive. I reached into my pocket and pulled out the DeFrancesco Diamond.

"Bower, listen to me. If you pull us out of this dive and promise to get us back to New York in one piece, the DeFrancesco Diamond is yours...$1.5 million, all yours."

Bower eyed the gem with considerable interest.

"$1.5 million?" he said.

I nodded.

"All mine?"

I nodded.

"It's a deal," he said, relieving me of the DeFrancesco Diamond that my mother had bequeathed to me.

He pulled the yoke back and pushed the throttle forward. The nose of the aircraft pointed up and we started to climb.

At the point that Bower pulled the 747 out of its kamikaze dive, we were so close to the *QEII* that I could read the mah-jongg tiles held in the fingers of women on the recreation deck.

When we landed at Kennedy, the aircraft was surrounded by heavily armed police and special agents. But instead of seizing Bower as I'd expected, I was arrested and charged with conspiracy to commit murder by destroying a cruise ship with a plummeting commercial aircraft, a federal offense. It was Bower's wiles and an unbelievable confluence of events that had successfully conspired against me. Apparently Olivia and her convict husband had been on the *QEII,* celebrating his unexpected parole. Bower and the federal authorities concocted a story that in a fit of jealousy, I attempted to bribe Bower with the DeFrancesco Diamond to crash the plane into the cruise ship, killing the woman who'd jilted me and wasting her loathsome beau. Bower even produced a parachute and an inflatable rubber raft that he claimed I'd supplied him, enabling him to escape the aircraft well before impact.

At the nationally televised tribunal, Olivia betrayed me. She presented detailed testimony that I was "essentially a bilious individual," that "beneath a mask of jocularity, [I] had *Schadenfreude* written all over [my] face."

My attorney, Gary Knobloch, put up a feeble defense, calling only one witness, my old boyhood chum Joaquin Royal, who under cross-examination claimed that I'd taken advantage of his color blindness when we shared crayons in the first grade.

Each member of the tribunal delivered a personal denunciation before sentencing me to death.

Scientists now believe that each person's "expiration date" is encoded within his or her DNA. They've located the operative genes on the operative chromosome and deciphered the specific sequencing of adenine, thymine, cytosine, and guanine that determine, from the moment of conception, an individual's life span. In other words, scientists are now convinced that it's possible to perform a DNA scan—something that will be as easy to do as a laser scan of the universal product code at the supermarket—and determine the exact date and time of day of an individual's death. The potential for abuse is enormous, of course. I remember speaking to a librarian who said that if a DNA scan shows that a person will die, say, on August 15th, and he or she wants to take out a book that's due on the 16th, then "we're just going to have to turn that person down." Well, I'd never had a DNA life-span scan, but it was obvious that my time had come.

As the date of my execution drew closer, there was trouble on death row. A convict was denied his last meal request—

bacon and eggs over easy, rye toast, and fries—because it exceeded the cholesterol limits set by the President's Penal Lifestyle and Wellness Task Force.

Luckily I'd developed an unusually close relationship with the warden. Knowing how much I loved Miës van der Rohe, he had an electric Barcelona chair custom-built for my execution. And when the date finally came and I was led into the death chamber, I couldn't help but marvel at the delicate curvature of the X-shaped legs, the perfect finish of the plated steel and the leather upholstery, and the magnificent, almost monumental proportions that have made the Barcelona chair timeless.

As the warden attached the electrodes to my body, I asked him if I could read a magazine. He gave me that week's issue of *Newsweek*, which had a photo of the president of the International Mensa Society on the cover. She was reaching up to her skull with both her hands, bending over, and spreading her cerebral hemispheres for the photographer.

And as I sat there with the electrodes attached to my head, perusing *Newsweek,* I couldn't help but recall those days back at the Wilford Military Academy of Beauty when we'd sit under the hair dryers at the training salon, flipping through our favorite magazines. And then my mind wandered to a particularly hot day at the Academy. We'd been standing under the brutal sun for hours as our drill instructor quizzed us.

"Unwanted facial hair?" he barked.

"Electrolysis, sir!" we chorused.

Well, here I am, sir. The most unwanted hair on the face of the earth.

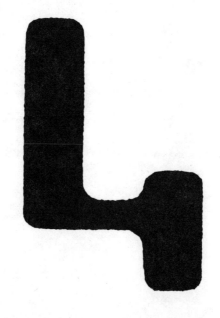

bathed in the cobalt radioluminescence of 10,000 ufo surveillance beams, aloisio de oliveira, rio de janeiro's most celebrated gastroenterologist/playboy languorously nuzzles the damp spicy baudelairean armpits of his 14-year-old lover arleen portada lead singer for brazil's most notoriously nihilistic samba band the nice maclords splayed hairlessly at the foot of a graffiti-splattered sliding pond   her bra is made out of french-fried potatoes with lacquered daubs of sweet brazilian ketchup at each nipple   it sells for well over 10,000 brazilian yen at rio's most fashionable boutiques

perhaps already i've said too much   on this lugubrious new year's eve, the goblets and demitasse cups piled so high as to obscure the faucet which drips methodically like a knuckle rapping methodically   he draws a line but the line is like a single hair which he can never brush from the page   drinking pineapple liquor and smoking marijuana

with the khmer rouge in the jungles of kampuchea, he felt. . .
suddenly neurotic   he was rarely seen in public without a
chic demoiselle on his arm, but that didn't stop him from feeling
like . . . something grown in a petri dish!

after the crafts fair, earl and kitty moseyed down to kitty's
place and got stinking drunk   cossell's a goop big earl said
lolling in a hammock that squeaked as it swayed back and forth
on kitty's porch   he knocked his hat back at a rakish tilt and
swigged the fiery hooch   you heard of bathtub gin well this
here's stall-shower mash big earl smirked   i lack vitality
emotion or warmth tonight admitted kitty but i am free from
pathogenic microorganisms   the extraordinary rococo
preciousness of big earl's needlepoint style created great
excitement at the crafts fair and his piece *the dallas cowboys in
israel* garnered the coveted *prix de gauguin*

it was "colonoscope nite" at the lucky stiff, new haven's
most notorious gay bar—gastroenterologists pay half price for
all kahlúa drinks until midnight   zelda dance critic for the
italian communist party daily *l'unita* italy's most contentious
newspaper bounced into the lucky stiff she never missed a
chance to judge the dance contest on "colonoscope nite"   the
best dancers win all-expense-paid trips to thighland a
mountainous kingdom in micronesia the size of tribeca where
they'll be honorary guests of the nice maclords at a royal
command performance for the king and queen of thighland
hyperpituitary giants who as custom decrees eschew toothpaste
and speak only in the french *passé simple*   all restaurants in
thighland offer ballet parking lanky black youths in fuchsia
tutus glissading into automobiles and gracefully backing into
rows that stretch elegantly to the sea   i've acquired a taste
for baboon meat sometimes i lie in bed all afternoon like colette
eating it straight from the can he said wanly   she measured
his penis with a shoe salesmen's metal slide   you're about a
size 7 zelda said

my horoscope predicts that on may 16th i will marry eddie
mustafa muhammad former wba light-heavyweight champion
she says wanly   i suffer from necropheliaphobia—a fear of
having sex with dead people he says wanly   who are the new
intellectuals who are the new aesthetes now that the old new
intellectuals and the old new aesthetes have been decimated
by the self-decimating ramifications of their old new ideas?
she asks wanly   he picks up a copy of *das plumpe denken*
new england's most disreputable german-language
newsmagazine   blast in egg cream factory kills
philatelist   he turns the page   radioactive glow-
in-the-dark semen found in canada   he turns the
page   cosmologist claims extraterrestrial maids visit earth
every wednesday   he turns the page   modern-day
hottentots carry young in resealable sandwich bags   he turns
the page   wayne newton calls mother's womb single-
occupancy garden of eden   morgan fairchild calls sally
struthers loni anderson

        when a mosquito bites your prick that's called a hoboken
blow job   in august the mosquitos of hoboken fall deliriously
in love with men's pricks   drunk with the miasmic froth that
floats across the hudson like *crème fraîche* the lovesick mosquitos
choose their mates haphazardly like the bleary-eyed anomic
patrons of a west side singles bar with conversational gambits
like i just finished playing two hours of racketball in a poorly
ventilated un-airconditioned building wearing a pair of
shetland wool panties and you have the same kind of vestal
physicality that makes the sears roebuck catalog, with its artless
spread of locker room lingerie, the world's premier stroke book
and i feel totally eroticized as if i'd been kidnapped by william
masters and virginia johnson sequestered in the wine cellars
of ernest and julio gallo and finally dumped in the pungent
laundry hamper of sylvester stallone where i forge a kind of
psychosexual tantric mind-lock with *el exigente* the demanding
one whose ability to keep me on the verge of reichian orgasmic
unconsciousness rivals nijinski's astonishing ability to pause at

the height of his jump complete the 1040 long form and float
softly to the ground

heck   you know me   my name's billy   my father
runs the vomitorium over on oakhurst and elm street   you
must have seen me a zillion times 'cause i cut through your
backyard on the way to school every day   heck   you must
know my mom too   y'ever see that commercial for the kung
fu institute of london where jean shrimpton and lord snowden
fend off a gang of skinheads with nunchakus? well that's my
mom doing the voice-over at the end   in new jersey call
201-795-3384   like freud, my dad referred affectionately to
his children as *fratzen* and *wormen*—brats and worms   one
sunday evening he pointed to a couple seated on the sofa and
said these are your godparents and in the event of a midair
collision or an outbreak of malaria that kills your poor mother
and myself you'll be remanded into the custody of these two
dear devoted friends who'll provide all the creature comforts a
creature like you deserves   i hated these two with a fervor
that very nearly imperiled my health   equally i loathed their
son whose cankerous smirk i can barely contemplate without
retching   here's a kid who decided between attending yale or
harvard by killing the family's irish wolfhound and reading its
entrails

he was consuming alcohol with the reckless avidity
of a hollywood indian   his hands were like the hands of
italian men caressing and pinching the cheeks of his own
behind   instead of putting kahlúa in his white russians the
bartender had mistakenly added maikua juice a powerful plant-
derived hallucinogen used by the jívaro tribesmen of the
eucadorian amazon   his head was a vegematic   he put a
cabbage in one ear and shook out coleslaw from the other   i
want to tell you something he said sullenly

i can't talk now i'm watching bruno hauptmann, bruno
hauptmann she says sullenly   i can't talk now i'm reading the

part of *blondie's himalayas* where dagwood resplendent in a
ceremonial fur-trimmed robe and dome-shaped gold brocade hat
has sleepwalked into the kitchen of the dalai lama's lhasa
fortress and topped off one of his famous late-night triple-tiered
sandwiches with a large oozy pat of yak butter she says
sullenly   i can't talk now i'm at the kentucky derby   four
horses are entered: the butler with a college education, carole
lombard says, basil blacknell otolaryngologist, and studying the
yanomamo   basil blacknell otolaryngologist is the odds-on
favorite, carole lombard says is the distant long shot, studying
the yanomamo and the butler with a college education are 6–2
and 7–5 bets respectively, she says sullenly   perhaps already
i've said too much, she says suddenly

     it was the night before the night before christmas   we
were all watching leni riefenstahl's documentary of the 1936
berlin olympics   bubbles eyed the screen quizzically, is
that a finn? she gesticulated   i like bubbles, she has a pair
of dice tattooed on her behind   pass the pindar said
rabbi gandelman reaching for a volume of the theban
poet   gandelman, a six-foot-six 275-lb. daddy warbucks
lookalike, is the first rabbi ever to score over 40 points in a
wheelchair basketball game   he refuses to marry although his
congregation has offered him a succession of voluptuous high-iq
virgins   something in the way the eastern european women
levitate themselves over the high-jump bar attracts me like no
other lover sang bubbles' husband the reverend humberto
perez   we are all watching how do you spell jew? a new
program produced by tennessee public television station
wkpt   each week a member of the tennessee state house of
representatives is sent back in time to meet a famous jew from
history   this week rep. jeeter maloney tennessee's youngest
state representative is sent back in history to rijnsburg, holland
to meet the metaphysical philosopher baruch spinoza judaism's
most notoriously heretical luminary   please have some
kuchen and coffee spinoza says   much obliged, drawls
maloney sampling the kuchen, ummmmmmm yum ... what did

you call these—cookin?   kuchen spinoza replies please help
yourself to more   i wonder how many of these kuchen you
could stuff into my mouth maloney wonders out loud   that's
something upon which i have often speculated spinoza says and
as maloney stretches his mouth wide open with both his hands
spinoza stuffs three and finally four kuchen in   there's a long
somewhat uncomfortable silence   i'm having a lot of trouble
lately with my son jeeter jr., maloney finally says, all he seems
to want to do is play video games   what are video games?
spinoza asks   as we leave rijnsburg its inhabitants are sitting
down to their customarily modest dinners of fish cakes and
room-temperature fresca and as the sun sets chattering black-
billed magpies lurch ungracefully into the cool tulip-scented
evening air   it is impossible to adequately describe my
feelings of utter resignation and pessimism as i scanned bubbles'
apartment and catalogued the moldering dishes of half-eaten
food, the psychotic mascara-caked mannequins, the album
covers and magazines tossed in a wild miscellany of intoxicated
carelessness, the moaning emaciated cats inhaling and exhaling
like bony accordions, the scampering roaches and silverfish, the
welch's grape juice bottle containing four ounces of liquid
pcp   but i like bubbles, she has a tiny naked smurf tattooed
between her breasts

    tonight at madison square garden the new york rangers
disemboweled the boston bruins' goalie, brought a hibachi onto
the ice, roasted his intestines and served them on toast points to
the howling hometown fans   my cousin my gastroenterologist
is himself in the hospital after having been viciously attacked at
a hawaiian luau   he's got three potentially dangerous ukulele
fragments lodged in his brain the doctor says jabbing at an x-
ray with his pointer

    i'm forging my new epic style in this dingy oubliette which
stinks   i mean the oubliette stinks not the style it stinks of
sulfur and bile and burnt rubber and putrescent flesh viz all
the ingredient odors of an epic style & of course i'm wearing

the very down-home the very tight alchemist's jeans and the
tempered industrial goggles   there is my beautiful mute
sister wheeling about the schoolyard like the last bright leaf of
autumn   a few hairs sprout from the crotch of her bikini
bottom   look at the paparazzi taking pictures of her!   oh
gaudy kitschy iridescent electroencephalogram of the insomniac
brain how i love you how i love you

      i want to tell you something but you're going to have to
come sit over here so i can whisper it in your ear because it's
extremely extremely confidential top secret information and if it
ever leaked out that i told you they'd kill me   who? (who'd
kill a sweet guy like you?)   the big boys would definitely
sit on my sunglasses with their asses   who are the big
boys?   the pope or the pope's valet de chambre i'm 99% sure
it would be one or the other   what's that poking out from the
top of your trousers it looks red and plastic   he clears throat
ah-hem ah-hem peels off awful smelly socks rolls them up and
tosses them into a crystal wassail bowl 2 points she's like a little
girl pulling at the leg of his trousers mister? mister? he's like
camus preoccupied with finding a good station on his car radio
and driving into a tree huh? where am i? he wakes up with a
start it's too dark to distinguish animal from vegetable they've
converted edison's *black maria* into a duplex come in i just
moved so all i can offer you is a cushion on the floor frozen
stolichnaya? decaffeinated tea? come sit over here so i can
whisper in your ear   it looks red and plastic   i was
visiting a netsilik eskimo in pelly bay whose name translated
into english means dental pulp or periodontal membrane
depending on one's glottal inflection and peggy lee called and
said i'm frantic they're showing the final scene of *knishing for
keeps* where peter minuit the ghost of wall street decrees that
those who labor with their minds shall rule those who grovel
with their hands and my tv's on the fritz so get over here right
away so i got in the car and burned up the interstate and i
stopped at a stuckey's and bought this red plastic dagger you
can feel it for a buck   that reminds me of what the comtesse

de la tour du pin said about louis the sixteenth: "his sword was
a perpetual embarrassment to him"   how lapidary i can see it
up in lights: HIS SWORD WAS A PERPETUAL EMBARRASSMENT
TO HIM   she turns on the television   the local news is
airing footage of bludgeoned birds   the police say the birds
were beaten with a seven-foot two-by-four a snow shovel and the
stump of a sassafras tree   what are you holding in your
hand?   the stump of a sassafras tree he says shaking his semi-
erect penis at her   not here not on the floor   if maria
theresa could give birth to marie antoinette in an armchair you
can certainly make love to me on the poop deck of the *black
maria*   if you're going to take me to bed you have to tell me a
bedtime story   ok there was a nauseating rotten-egg odor in
the air and mr. and mrs. becker walked to the jewelry store
with clothespins on their noses   we'd like a lovely pendant
for our daughter judith   judith is a very brilliant girl they
boasted   a very sweet girl an honest girl an attractive
girl   later while mrs. becker was prostrate on the floor
as flat as a pancake as if she'd been run over by a steamroller the
jeweler psychoanalyzed mr. becker   why do you fear sexual
intercourse so mr. becker   i have a number of cysts on my
penis mr. becker said and i'm hesitant about engaging in sexual
relations with women because i'm scared that they'll think these
cysts are venereal warts or tumors   don't be silly the jeweler
said the cysts will make intercourse all the more enjoyable for
the women   i'll show you   they went to the four seasons a
very elegant restaurant on east fifty-second street in manhattan
they sat down at a table and the jeweler opened up a copy of
screw magazine to a page advertising dildos and vibrators and
french ticklers and sure enough many of the devices were
bumpy textured rough gnarled jagged   see said the
jeweler women pay for bumpy penises it makes it better for
them   mr. becker looked at the jeweler the jeweler looked at
mr. becker it was a moment of intense gratification for both
men   we have a good relationship with each other mr. becker
said   the jeweler nodded earnestly   yes we do   later
they went to the rodeo   have one of mine the jeweler said

offering becker a cigarette   have one of mine becker
said   no have one of mine said the jeweler   no have one of
mine becker said   have one of mine said the jeweler   all
right stop i want you to start loving me now but please do
me one favor i want you to refer to my vagina as the jack
teagarden pavilion in other words when the time comes and it's
appropriate you'll say for instance i like the feel of your jack
teagarden pavilion i like the smell of your jack teagarden
pavilion   this is the moment of ecstasy?   oh yes this is the
moment of ecstasy   the ornamental tin rooster with large
beady eyes of amber glass exploding in the jack teagarden
pavilion   what part of me do you feel   the part where
samson kills a thousand philistines with the jawbone of an
ass   what is the peculiar sound of our coitus   the sound of
arriving in sainte-anne de beaupré the land of lonesome pines
where every night is moo shu pork night via dog sled   the
sound of three elderly spinster sisters whispering in a movie
theatre in pointe-au-pic a small resort along the north shore of
the saint lawrence river frequented by the 300-lb. president
william taft   yes   the sound of sabbatai zevi sinking his
scepter into the gooey terra firma of seventeenth-century
turkey   the folk music of flu season recorded by the
ethnomusicologist with no name   the concerto for comb and
tinfoil based upon the moment i was conceived in my mother's
womb the shrill dissonance of a korean lullaby the ludicrous
billing and cooing of an uxurious husband the yodeling
shanties of marat in his tub   you are my teething
ring   my birdbath   my litter box   my abominable
snowmobile   my sizzling electric chair   my not-so-sweet
donkey kong!   they pant in a crescendo of inflammatory
climactic epithets   once upon a time there was a man and a
woman who had just finished making love she whispers absently
entwining her fingers in the slack webbing of his lacrosse stick
and they felt as if they were floating, like cafeteria trays in a
space capsule, like secretaries in a pool   the sex had made
him feel strong and rugged like harry morgan in hemingway's
to have and have not and he went to his typewriter and wrote:

this is real tough macho autobiography, the kind shelley winters
writes when she recounts biting the head off a mallard duck
at the bear river migratory bird refuge in utah, a real
premenstrual stunt, but i'm not interested in that gary gilmore
hit-me-with-your-best-shot stuff anymore, fish are my central
motif, goldfish, clams on the half shell, dolphin kinship
structures, sole almondine, i'm trying to write a piece called the
aesthetics of surface for an israeli semiotics journal for 500
israeli pounds, but i'm under the deadline gun, jack   i'm
putting lines of 99% pure bogotá cocaine up my nose, i'm
filling my enema bag with tequila   i'm trying to get at the
shimmering patina on the filmy superstratum of the surface, but
i'm having wrenchingly vivid flashbacks of my mother flaying
my thighs with an antenna   i had to fight my way through
workingclass polish neighborhoods every day on the way to
the kidney dialysis unit   it's rough, man, but i'm a rough
super-macho motherfucker, jack   i swagger around saying
fuck you man, kiss my white ass, suck my hickory-smoked
dick!   i'm saying things like chacun à son gout oedipus rex,
you schmuck   but the sex had made her feel hostile and
resentful that she had been cajoled and manipulated into losing
control and exposing her passion to a virtual stranger   men
aren't worth the paper they're printed on she said and she
grabbed his penis with both her hands and swung him over her
head like an olympic hammer thrower and flung him through the
living room window into a slow elliptical orbit around the earth
and the russians thought he was american and the americans
thought he was russian but we all knew that he was just a
hapless naked man tumbling through space whose orbit once
every year would bring him close enough to dayton ohio for
schoolchildren there to discern his wistful fleeting hello good-bye,
hello good-bye, hello good-bye

enter the squirrel

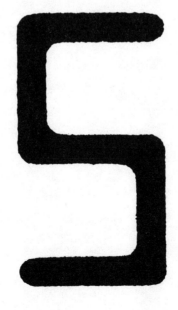

H e'd never shot a woman before. He'd shot men, plenty of them. Shot them, bludgeoned them, garroted them, drowned them, poisoned them, he'd even pushed some poor slob out of a 747 as he crapped in his pants and pleaded for his life. But he'd never shot a woman before. No, wait a minute. He had shot a woman before. There was that dance therapist in Fort Lauderdale. He'd filled her with so much lead you could have sharpened her head and done a crossword puzzle with her. He'd shot women before but never anyone as beautiful as this. He'd never shot a beautiful woman before, that's it. And this one was beautiful, wow. Long legs, long long hairy prehensile toes. An ape-woman. Square peg teeth, hairy floppy ears, a bridgeless nose with wide flattened nostrils. He'd never shot an ape-woman before. Well, come to think of it, he had shot an ape-woman. Back in '63 in Reno. But he'd never shot an ape-woman this beautiful. Nope.

...Where was I? muses Big Squirrel, reloading his pistol. Oh yeah...don't forget, put plenty of duck sauce on the egg rolls. One of the kids in the audience stands up. Big Squirrel, you forgot to put the egg rolls in the microwave. All the kids in the audience start to giggle. Big Squirrel, you're so silly, they chime, hysterical with giggles, you're a big silly, you can't eat egg rolls when they're frozen! Big Squirrel fires a warning shot in the air. It's time for yoga! he says. Yea! yea! go the kids. OK, how many of you have accumulated mucus in your lower bowel? Yea! yea! Yogi Vithaldas, come out here. The organist plays a few bars of snake charmer music. Kids, give Yogi Vithaldas a nice Big Squirrel hello. Howdy, Yogi Vithaldas, they chime. Hello, kids. Yogi Vithaldas, tell the kids out there a little bit about yourself. Well, I just got married, Bill. Did you hear that, kids?! Yea! yea! Yup...my beautiful wife is a psychic who specializes in mediumistic psychotherapy—say you're in the middle of psychoanalysis and your analyst dies—you don't want to have to forage through upper Manhattan for someone new and start all over again at square one in the uterus—so my wife will conduct a séance and contact your late-lamented analyst in the spirit world: knock once for libido fixation, twice for obsessive-compulsion neurosis. And my brother-in-law is a movie star—y'know that Japanese film *In the Realm of the Senses* where the woman cuts off her lover's penis and walks around Tokyo for four days with it in her pocket—well, my brother-in-law played the penis. And the three of us are honeymooning at the beautiful Beijing Buena Vista Motel where we'll play mah-jongg with Madame Jiang Qing and toast the memory of Mao Zedong with hundred-year-old egg creams. Yea! Mazel tov, Yogi Vithaldas, now what do you have for us today? Today I have a yogic bowel cleansing exercise that can save you kids a lot of big gastroenterologist bills. Yogi Vithaldas assumes the graceful lotus pose. Without warning, Big Squirrel screams, It's kung fu time! and leaping high into the air delivers an explosive roundhouse kick upside Yogi Vithaldas's head that sends his right eyeball flying into a Styrofoam coffee cup. Olé! go the kids. OK, kids, today we have rare footage of lions eating a Christian taken by an amateur photographer at the Colosseum in 290 A.D. As the grainy, flickering footage appears on the studio monitor, Big Squirrel comes backstage to towel off. I approach Big Squirrel at the Pepsi machine. Big Squirrel, you are the world's most formidable master of Tiger and Crane style kung fu. Walid Jumblatt's Druse Militiamen are heading for the U.S.A. We need your lethal and balletic Tiger and Crane style kung fu to defeat and slaughter Walid Jumblatt's Druse Militiamen. What is your answer? Big Squirrel stares mystically into his Pepsi. I hear the twang of a chest hair being plucked, he says. (What Big Squirrel say mean Big Squirrel help fight Walid Jumblatt's Druse Militiamen.)

I'm dialing numbers frantically, fingers flying over push buttons in a blur, in my ear a crazy cacophony of electronic beeps. I'm getting places like Wales, Sterling Colorado, Vladivostok, Altamont Speedway, Barnes & Noble Annex, Nuremberg, Braintree Mass., and Biafra. I'm stirring a pitcher of Tanqueray martinis with one hand and sliding a tray of frozen clams *oreganata* into the oven with my foot. I've got a dozen cigarettes going simultaneously in ashtrays all over the apartment. God, these Methedrine suppositories that Yogi Vithaldas gave me are good! As I iron a pair of tennis shorts I dictate a haiku into the tape recorder and then dash off to snake a clogged drain in the bathroom sink and then do three minutes on the speedbag before making an origami praying mantis and then reading an article in *High Fidelity* magazine as I stir the coq au vin. These Methedrine suppositories are fantastic! I'm spinning through the apartment like a whirling dervish, finishing things I'd put off for months, cleaning the venetian blinds, defrosting the freezer, translating *The Ring of the Nibelung* into Black English, gluing a model aircraft carrier together for my little son. I'm writing to my congressman, doing push-ups, changing a light bulb as I floss my teeth and feed my fish with one hand, balance my checkbook with the other and scratch my borzoi's silky stomach with my big toe. The stimulatory effect of the suppositories is convulsive. I'm an

exploding skeleton of kinetic vectors. I stand upon a peak in
Darien like stout Cortez shouting I write the songs! I rupture
into afterimages like the nude descending a staircase.
Holographic clones of myself appear all over the apartment
smoking cigarettes and drinking martinis. Where are the
women, they chuckle. Mona arrives to borrow a cup of sugar.
Quaaludes. Clothes shed. Gang bang. Death. Ambulance. Police.
Apartment a mess. Next morning call maid. Maid arrives,
drinks martinis, swallows goldfish, and vomits on little son. I
take a deep breath...

    The omens are inauspicious. In my haunted closet,
mothballs mysteriously assemble into a triangle like a rack of
billiard balls, my pants wriggle from their hangers and dance
the cancan. Each night I have the same dream: I'm sitting on
the john in the men's room at Avery Fisher Hall—at the climax
of Rimsky-Korsakov's *Scheherezade* a swordfish flies up out of the
toilet water and buries itself in my rectum, but when I look
down into the bowl I find that in actuality I've defecated the
missing 18-minute section of Watergate tape. Each morning I
wake up on the ledge of a tall building gripping the concrete
with white fingernails. In kindergartens and pediatric waiting
rooms, young children greet each other with handshakes and
eerily formal salutations. Whales throw themselves on the decks
of whaling ships with interminable Schopenhauerian suicide
notes pinned to their dorsal fins. The Puerto Rico Day parade is
the largest in history, it is visible even to the astronauts who
point excitedly from the porthole of their orbiting space shuttle,
but tragedy strikes when the parade's grand marshal Herman
Badillo bludgeons himself to death with his own ceremonial
scepter after learning that his mother's gynecologist was aboard
the ill-fated Korean jetliner flight #007. My mother wanders
around the house like a member of the Manson family, saying
"Maalox is groovy" and when I ask her to explain she says that
the mucilaginous remains of history's cannibalized explorers
from Magellan to David Rockefeller have collected in her
stomach like wads of undigested chewing gum, giving her
terrific heartburn, she says that she has a huge hair ball in her

stomach made of the exquisitely flaxen underarm hair of Amelia
Earhart. Cupping my ear to a bowl of Rice Krispies I hear
German V-2 rockets falling on London Bridge. Unemployed
laboratory mice laid off after cuts in federal research funding
huddle in skid row alleyways guzzling miniature bottles of
airline whiskey. When the president finds out that the
astronauts left a new popularized version of the Bible on the
moon instead of leaving the King James he is outraged. He calls
an emergency meeting of the Girl Scouts and the Teamsters
Union. In that Bible, he fumes, Delilah uses Nair on Samson's
head and Jesus Christ is crucified with Phillips-head screws and
Krazy Glue. He makes the astronauts go back to the moon and
switch Bibles. But there is another snafu and this time instead
of leaving the King James Bible on the moon they leave Cecil
Brown's novel, *The Life and Loves of Mr. Jiveass Nigger.*
Two elderly chimpanzees who, in the heyday of television
documentaries about primate speech capacity, required
sumptuous private dressing rooms with stars on the doors, now
sit dejectedly in a Miami Beach Laundromat using sign
language to bemoan their dwindling pensions and persistent
hemorrhoids. Moving men hoist a Soviet-made antiaircraft
rocket launcher into the third-floor window of a Beirut
brownstone. Put it right next to the chifforobe, says Wali
Assam, coyly raising her veil. Wali Assam is Beirut's most
celebrated sexual self-help authoress. Her latest volume,
Liquidating the Zionist Entity in the Nude, is number one on
the best-seller list. Please don't make me move the chifforobe,
says one of the workmen. Which one of you grungy hunks has
the biggest muscle, she says, undulating the ruby in her navel.
Don't flirt with the workmen! bellows a stentorian voice that
rattles the china. Who is that? demands Wali Assam. This is
your kitchen drain speaking! Don't flirt with the workmen! An
enormous Caucasian fat man in plaid Bermuda shorts spraying
Windex on the front windshield of a Datsun 280-Z with a
Playboy rabbit dangling from the rearview mirror gets a cramp
and calls out, Grandma! Grandma! Vultures circle above. The
scene is worse at Bergdorf Goodman's: frenzied women in estrus

writhe on their bellies in the aisles, mooing, snorting, and
ululating, clutching violently at their breasts and loins. In an
effort to quell the feral cravings of the super-horny shoppers,
Abolhassan Bengazzara, the reptilian sadist and Savak alumnus
who commands the notorious Bergdorf Goodman's internal
security police, orders his men to load their weapons with darts
containing powerful doses of Librium and testosterone. Me
and Huck are trapped in a fitting room in the junior miss
department. Every time one of us pokes his head out a dart
comes whizzing by. You don't want to get hit with one of those
darts, says Huck, they'll make you sleepy and your balls'll swell
up like muskmelons. During a lull in the shooting Huck goes
foraging for food and returns with a bag of Famous Amos
cookies, a pocketful of papaya jelly beans, and a box of frozen
tortellini. Later by the campfire Huck reclines with his ukulele
and sings love songs to his girlfriend in Hannibal. When ten-
story radiation-spawned mutant leviathans rise from the
bubbling slime of toxic cesspools, tossing their ophidian manes
of napalm-spouting lymph tubes, the U.S. Air Force will shower
them with hydrogen bombs but don't cry, little love bug, after
the mushroom cloud clears we'll be eating cream of mushroom
soup in Monte Carlo, where the manhole covers are embossed
with champagne glasses & bubbles and the gendarmes are armed
with party favors, croons Huck. Huck is heavily into a Bertolt
Brecht/Barbra Streisand thing. Later we go to the Thalia and
sit through a double feature of *Mother Courage* and *Yentl*.
During the climactic scene in *Yentl* where Barbra Streisand
eats 300 salted herrings to prove to the other rabbinical
students that she is macho, Huck weeps uncontrollably and
vomits.

That night Walid Jumblatt's Druse Militiamen roll into
town, gunning the engines of their Harley-Davidson 1200s,
firing celebratory bursts from their Kalishnikov assault rifles into
the sky, their flamboyant phosphorescent nylon djellabas
streaming behind them like the wind-whipped ensigns of a
buccaneer raiding ship as teenage girls, roused from their
slumber by the pungent pheromones that waft from the armpits
of the hell-bent Moslems on wheels, emerge from between their

crisply creased sheets and pastel quilts, insert their diaphragms and plugs of spermicide, garnish their faces with cherry-red lipstick and lavender eye shadow, slip into tight capri pants, flimsy halter tops, and gem-studded slave bracelets, and flock somnambulantly to the local bar as if bitten by vampires.

Over decaffeinated espresso in his tersely appointed Gramercy Park apartment-cum-atelier, I chatted with Big Squirrel as he packed his valise in preparation for battle with the Druse Militiamen. Ball-bearing swivel nunchaku. Check. Black vinyl zippered nunchaku carrying case. Check. Ninja hood. Check. Ninja throwing stars. Check. Long-handled broadsword. Check. Butterfly knives. Check. Protective groin cup. Check. Big Squirrel executed a reverse aerial somersault onto the coffee table, scissoring my head between his knees. I involuntarily spit a hot stream of decaffeinated espresso into his lap. Our eyes met. It was a moment of intense spiritual communion. I want you to promise that if anything happens to me you'll see that my wife gets this, Big Squirrel said, waving the protective groin cup in my face. Please repeat the aforementioned, Big Squirrel, the viselike grip of your knees is causing considerable static along my auditory nerve path in addition to cutting off the vital flow of blood to my cerebral cortex and thalamic receptor nodes. Big Squirrel relaxed his hold and reiterated his solemn request. Listen, man, I said, I love my country. And I swear to you, Big Squirrel, that if you fall in battle I will personally deliver this protective groin cup to your bereaved wife. Thank you, said Big Squirrel, it was given to me as a wedding present by my father-in-law, chief of the Poznaks—a moody and fiercely independent tribe which inhabits a coastal plateau of Northeastern Ethiopia. The tribal truss-maker fashioned it from the bony carapace of a mud turtle. The Poznaks are an ingeniously resourceful people who subsist entirely on hot dogs, using the frankfurter skins for clothing, mashing the minced filling along with manioc tubers to make the glutinous pulp which is the staple of their diet, decocting the juice of the frankfurter and using the psychotropic distillate in their shamanistic rituals, and dipping the sharpened points of ossified hot dogs in curare and shooting them from their blowguns. Their magnificent cave paintings of picnicking Poznaks, meticulously stippled in the red sticky sweat of hippopotami, anticipated the pointillism of Georges Seurat by thousands of years. The Poznaks taught me many esoteric and deadly styles of kung fu including the 5 Plum, the Phoenix Eye, and the Jade Claw, and also Deli Style kung fu. Big Squirrel sighed heavily and averted his eyes. When my wife left her people in Ethiopia and returned with me to the U.S.A. she was very homesick and cried for weeks and weeks. She was unable to acclimate herself to this culture. She became irritable and I often had to resort to my most powerful kung fu to subdue her tantrums. As time went on she became increasingly despondent, listless, and withdrawn. I'd come home and find her washing barbiturates down with tumblers full of whiskey. Her sadness was breaking my heart, it was murdering me. Finally, upon the advice of my cousin, chief of gastroenterology at Mount Sinai, I had my wife committed to the Chef Boy-Ar-Dee Institute of Psychiatry. There psychiatrists told me that it was essential that my wife eat tremendous amounts of Italian food if there was to be any hope of her ever leading a normal life. They said that since Mussolini's invasion of Ethiopia they'd seen this condition in many of their Ethiopian patients. Throughout their formative years their parents ceaselessly revile Italian people and culture. The children in time come to associate their parents' derogation of Italy with parental derogation of themselves, resulting in increasingly bitter episodes of masochistic self-appraisal and ultimately functional ego death. By gradually introducing small amounts of Italian food into the diet of an Ethiopian adult, the psychiatrists are exploiting precisely those crossed wires which are buried deeply in the associative processes of the patient who has a desperate subconscious need to eat and enjoy Italian cuisine, thereby correspondingly revivifying his or her own sense of self-worth. Because of the severity of my wife's condition, doctors recommended a massive infusion of Italian food into her diet. Antipasto, pasta fagioli, and manicotti for breakfast. Ziti, ravioli, and chicken cacciatore for lunch. Fried calamari, stromboli, veal scaloppine, chicken parmigiana, and linguini in white clam sauce for dinner. And tremendous amounts of Chianti, Soave Bolla, espresso coffee, cannoli, and spumoni between meals. Tears welled in Big Squirrel's eyes and rolled down his cheeks. I held him in my arms as I'd never held a man before. Hush now, Big Squirrel, I said softly, I'll see that she gets the protective groin cup. I'll see that she gets the protective groin cup. I'll see that she gets the protective groin cup. . . .

After Big Squirrel's nap we went to a place called the Coal Hole, a restaurant on the Upper West Side located in an old coal mine. You take an elevator car about 300 ft. underground to the dining room. It's pitch dark and everyone wears one of those hard hats with the attached spotlight. Most of the waiters have black lung disease. It was the last restaurant Mimi Sheraton reviewed before quitting the *Times* and having her jaw wired shut. The dining room was extremely warm. I ordered a Tab. Big Squirrel ordered a Pepsi. There was an extraterrestrial serenity in Big Squirrel's face as Dionne Warwick's "Do You Know the Way to San Jose" wafted over the PA system. Do you really love Tab? he asked. He didn't wait for a reply. I think Tab tastes like raw sewage, he said. Big Squirrel, when you go off on what may be your final mercenary operation, there'll be a lot of people pulling for you. Do you have any parting words of advice for all the kids out there? If you want to be successful in life, he said, everything you do must be an act of patricide. You must always kill the father. Every song you sing, every sentence you write, every leaf you rake must kill the father. Every act from the most august to the most banal must be patricidal if you hope to live freely and unencumbered. Even when shaving—each whisker you shave off is your father's head. And if you're using a twin blade—the first blade cuts off the father's head and as the father's neck snaps back it's cleanly lopped off by the second blade.

The heat in the dining room had become unbearable. My gauzy flesh billowed like loose fabric in the hot drafts. And Big Squirrel's tattoo ran in lurid rivulets down his chest.

the suggestiveness of one stray hair

in an otherwise perfect coiffure

H e's got a car bomb. He puts the key in the ignition and turns it—the car blows up. He gets out. He opens the hood and makes a cursory inspection. He closes the hood and gets back in. He turns the key in the ignition. The car blows up. He gets out and slams the door shut disgustedly. He kicks the tire. He takes off his jacket and shimmies under the chassis. He pokes around. He slides back out and wipes the grease off his shirt. He puts his jacket back on. He gets in. He turns the key in the ignition. The car blows up, sending debris into the air and shattering windows for blocks. He gets out and says, Damn it! He calls a tow truck. He gives them his AAA membership number. They tow the car to an Exxon station. The mechanic gets in and turns the key in the ignition. The car explodes, demolishing the gas pumps, the red-and-blue Exxon logo high atop its pole bursting like a balloon on a string. The mechanic steps out. You got a car bomb, he says. The man rolls his eyes. I know that, he says.

the human bomb is ticking
the handsome blond robotic bomb with the gorgeous pecs and
    the cleft in his chin and the cute mustache is purring: tick
    tock tick tock tick tock
he puts a pinch of smokeless tobacco between his cheek and gum
    and watches a monarch butterfly mince gingerly across the
    hot hood of his idling chevy malibu
and little lovely winged electric razors hover about his head,
    gently kissing it until he is bald—and he dreams of john
    audubon and his lovely watercolor hummingbirds and his
    lovely watercolor chrysanthemums—though, unbeknownst
    to the human bomb, the ceramic cranium developed for
    him by japanese high-tech ceramics engineers to protect
    his brain is beginning to crack, so that really his
    watercolor dream of john audubon is not a dream at all
    but an aberrant pattern of electrical discharge generated
    by moisture seeping through the fissures in his glazed skull

and unbeknownst to the human bomb, he's been tampered with
    by terrorists who've rigged his detonator to his prostate
    gland, so the instant he ejaculates—*boom!*

it is autumn
and i am remembering autumn nights long ago when we
    watched those early episodes in which the handsome
    human bomb was motionlessly posed in the men's
    department at macy's in a van heusen cream-colored
    button-down, pierre cardin pin-dot lamb's wool tie, a nut-
    brown ralph lauren shetland wool sweater, stanley blacker
    corduroy sport coat, and bass weejun tassel-front brown
    leather slip-ons regularly $68 now on sale for $54.40
you were just a flag twirler at pocahontas high in mahwah
it was homecoming night when i met you
i remember you giggling shyly at the seniors bobbing for veal
    medallions in a metal basin of marsala sauce
you smelled of lilacs
that night we learned that ecstasy means the collapse of time
past present future perceived in a single instant
you were watching the trajectory of your own words as they left
    your mouth
words which disappeared into the horizon
words which, due to the curvature of space, returned many
    years later like murmuring boomerangs to your ear
you looked like an italian starlet—jet-black hair in a thick
    braid down your back, sloe-eyes set deeply above high
    cheekbones, olive complexion, full sensuous lips, the strap
    of your nightgown fallen languorously off your shoulder,
    mascara smeared, your eyelids heavy with drowsiness,
    your hair now spread across the pillow like a trellis of
    vines, your voice low and husky, your breath still redolent
    of anisette
and tonight as we watch television on the porch
your buckteeth seem shellacked in the cadmium light of the
    harvest moon

look at the screen

that's me with the amulets and anaconda pelts and the saucer-
size lip plug distending my mouth

that's me crouched in the backseat of the human bomb's chevy
malibu with his chubby friend ulrike grunebaum

though, without the proper software, ulrike grunebaum is like
mrs. potato head—without eyes, ears, nose, or mouth,
without id or libido, without creed or lineage—a
featureless and vacant globe of flesh

but with the proper software, she is ulrike grunebaum, the
chillingly eloquent marxist ideologue and machiavellian
technocrat in a gray three-piece suit and red necktie,
ruthlessly purging the upper echelons of her ruling
politburo

with the proper software, she is ulrike grunebaum, executive
curator of the jimi hendrix museum in baden-baden

and with the proper software—with a twist of the joystick—she
is ulrike grunebaum, the hamburg erotic-film queen whose
screen credits include *smell me tomorrow, the edible
fixation, we'll be nude at noon,* and *the odyssey of gomer*

we're taste-testing four varieties of lebanese halvah: druse,
phalangist, sunni, and shiite

the flecks of shrapnel in the phalangist halvah give it an
unusually nutty flavor

we're doing our cellulite exercises; we're doing the nine or ten
beautifully firming things you can do for your derriere

they're showing the video we made together for mtv in which i
play the naughty con ed man who's been discovered by
ulrike rummaging through her laundry hamper, sniffing
her brassieres, and ulrike wraps her prehensile eyelashes
around my delicate reed of a penis and slowly and
erotically strangles it until its head is the brilliant red of
autumn sumac leaves

when i put my ear against ulrike's temple, i can glean her
thoughts—because her thoughts are transmitted in the
morse code of her pulsing arteries

the human bomb throws his hot dog in the bushes

i'm about to say something horrible, something horribly
      unchristian...and please don't start singing, because no
      amount of mouthwash can camouflage the foul breath of
      hymn-singing christians...

this is my horrible statement: there's mustard in the bushes

your eyes follow the squiggle of yellow mustard to an ant who's
      about to be squashed beneath a shiny tooled-leather tony
      lama cowboy boot and the ant looks directly into the
      camera and says in yiddish with english subtitles, "i want
      to live as much as you do"—and this image traumatizes
      the country in the 1980s as much as the image of my head
      rolling from the guillotine saying, "i'm sorry, mommy, i'll
      be good" traumatized the country in the 1960s

i am on every channel and that infuriates you

that i have the ability to jump out of the television screen,
      burrow into your uterus, and emerge nine months later
      tan and rested bugs you very much

you're using the violent vocabulary of the u.s.a., you're violently
      chewing your cheez doodles and flicking the remote control

a computer programmer and mother of two from bethesda,
      maryland, puts her fingers through the holes in my head
      and bowls me

i'm rolling through roanoke, city of rheumatism and alzheimer's
      disease; through memphis, city of ulcerated tongues and
      saliva turned bitter and glutinous; through pine bluff,
      whose inhabitants store the ashes of their cremated dead in
      those white cardboard cartons with thin metal handles
      made for chinese takeout food; through shreveport, whose
      population lacks the enzyme necessary to break down
      spaghetti

i appear on the phil donahue show with other children of
      parents who'd had unsuccessful tubal ligations and
      vasectomies

my path connects every dot in texas

—oh dear, i'm quite lost; kind sir, can you tell me where i am?

—my, you're a peculiar sight, young man, you're balding but so
pretty, are you gay?

—no, sir, i have a cute girlfriend at home who is waiting for
me; please tell me where i am and lend me a quarter so i
can call home and reassure my sweetheart that i have not
been slain

—i am ordinarily the very soul of munificence, young friend,
but today you find me rather strapped for cash or coin...
perhaps in lieu of this phone call you will retire with
me to a public lavatory and i will initiate you into the
splendors of synchronized swimming

—i repeat with all respect, sir, that i am not homosexual; who
are you, sir, and ... who are you?

—i am not an octopus or a hen

—that i can see ... nor a crayfish

(later)

—things didn't, did they? i mean turn out the way you expected

—no, i was incapable of accepting my mother's death and i
frantically embraced fundamentalist judaism because
i refused to accept a world in which people were so
completely vulnerable and so capriciously and arbitrarily
victimized, i refused to endorse the purposelessness
and the randomness and i rushed into the arms of the
paternalistic teleological belief system of my ancestors, of
my parents, the very same judaism i'd so contemptuously
eschewed my whole life—but even my newfound
jewishness was fugitive

—how tall were you before your mother passed away?

—i was five-seven

—and the day after your mother passed away?

—four-one

—and today?

—today i am eight inches in diameter

—it sounds like you're going to disappear
—no, i'm in a perpetual state of contraction and expansion; now
     i'm contracting and just as i'm about to become smaller
     than anything, smaller than even the most infinitesimal
     subatomic particle, i'll begin to expand and i'll expand and
     expand and expand until there's literally no more room for
     me in the universe and my head is knocking against the
     ceiling of the space-time continuum and then i'll start to
     contract again and so on and so forth

i'm rolling down the pacific coast of south america, but i never
     make it to tierra del fuego
i'm a gutter ball
i was made in hong kong
i have reached a level of unparalleled ugliness—revolting
     bloated oily ugliness which has metastasized across every
     square inch of my body
sexual relations are impossible—i am hopelessly ugly, hopelessly
     silly
masturbation is impossible—my penis shrivels at my own touch
     and i lack the most minimal powers of poetic imagination
     necessary to conjure autoerotic fantasies
my gastrointestinal tract is listed as a must-to-avoid in the
     michelin guide for intestinal parasites
wherever i am at the moment is the remotest frontier of the
     diaspora

six flags, each depicting a still-frame from the zapruder film,
     flutter above dealey plaza
and diffracted shards of sunlight impale the ornamental carp
     who cough little bubbles of blood which cluster above the
     pond's mosaic floor whose tiles of azure and crimson depict
     an exploding head of ideas
as nearby, at james dean memorial hospital, nurses use cold
     bottles of milk to cool the perspiring brows of surgeons
     who are engraving ideas into the smooth tabula rasa
     brains of fetuses

an idea being that which exists at the moment a fly ball pauses at
    the apex of its flight and bids the sky adieu...
that moment is pregnant
perhaps at that moment, in an s&m bar in plymouth,
    massachusetts, the 50-ft. woman straddles your face and
    defecates 17,000 scrabble letters, fertilizing the fallow
    fields of your imagination...
and a new american style is born

when dawn came it was as if we'd been delivered stillborn from
    an assembly line
identically curled in our bed
our arms crooked in perfect symmetry beneath our pillows
we were like twin fossils
two tipsy vertebrates who had crawled into a tar pool in the
    wee hours of the pleistocene and slept through the tumult
    of history
in our mouths the rich creamy taste and texture of raw sea
    urchins, our breath was rank and aquatic
i pushed the hair from her forehead and her face was taut and
    limned in shadow like a death mask

when the forensic pathologists performed their autopsy on you
they cried, those hardened professionals,
because peeling the skin from your head
was like peeling the skin from an onion

the flesh between your breasts
was a thin and pasty dough
which yielded easily to their scalpels

and the forensic pathologists, those hardened professionals,
shook their fists at the photographs of the 10 most wanted men,
one of whom murdered you, and wept

oh amy, what threnody matters
in a world whose software

enables a crossword puzzle, orphaned by your death,
to ask, "who now will do me?"

i am not roller-skating through piles of brittle autumn leaves
i am roller-skating down the aisles at macy's in narcotic slow
      motion to the music of john philip sousa
i'm skating past every surveillance camera
i'm skating across every closed-circuit television screen
salesmen come and go, murmuring, "jerry lewis est mort…jerry
      lewis est mort"
if only i had the software to conjure one macy's salesgirl at the
      end of this endless corridor into whose arms i'd roller-skate
      deliriously to the optimistic cornets of john philip sousa
but i don't have the appropriate software
and it would be brainless to continue skating

in the kingdom of boredom,
i wear the royal sweatpants

I finally lost my patience and shrieked:
Get out, get out, all of you! My little
bedroom was filled with pilgrims, militants, hostages, clerics,
extremists, dissidents, mediators, ideologues, pragmatists, and
militiamen. If you're all not out of here in ten minutes, I'll have
a light-infantry unit equipped with armored personnel carriers
and artillery in here so fast it'll make your heads spin. Now out,
move it! My ultimatum was punctuated by the *boom boom boom*
of BM-13 multiple-rocket launchers and the whistling sound of
rising missiles. I pointed to a bunch of jerks standing near my
bookcases—these guys had really bugged me. They'd been
continuously making derisive wisecracks at my expense. At
night they noisily sucked on sour balls, making it impossible for
me to sleep, and they were either actually selling crack to my
little brother or attempting to induce my little brother to start
using crack. I want you guys identified and then blindfolded
and shackled and driven in buses to special interrogation
centers—now! A burly fanatic committed suicide soon after he

surrendered, biting into a cyanide capsule that had been hidden
in a ring on his right hand. His friends leveled accusatory looks
at me, as if I were somehow responsible for his death. I don't
care, it was his choice, I don't have the patience for this shit
anymore, everybody out! We can't leave, someone said. Why?
There's a river between here (he pointed to a spot on the map)
and our ancestral homeland, there (he pointed again), and the
river is too deep to ford. Yes, yes, mumbled his compatriots, too
deep to ford. You'll find portable pontoon bridges in my bureau
in the second drawer from the bottom.... Take them and shove
off. An old man with a gray beard edging his craggy face and
a leather bandolier of ammunition around his shoulder was
gesturing belligerently at another old man. What's the trouble?
I asked. He took my AK-47 assault rifle. I walked up to the other
old man and sure enough he had two AK-47s. Give him back his
AK-47 and I want you both out of here, and be quiet when you
pass my parents' room, I don't want them waking up, do you
understand? Now we're getting somewhere, I said to myself as
people starting clearing out. Okay, there's a 75-millimeter
Chinese-made recoilless rifle and a Soviet-made ZU-23
antiaircraft gun in the hallway near the bathroom—whom do
they belong to? A guy raised his hand: They belong to my
paramilitary security force. All right, I want you, your
paramilitary security force, the recoilless rifle, and the
antiaircraft gun out of here, and be extremely careful taking
the stuff downstairs—that's an antique walnut banister. A
young Air Force cadet approached me, saluting. Sir, do you
know where I can catch a B-1 bomber to New York, sir? What
airport, cadet, there's Kennedy, LaGuardia, and Newark. Sir,
LaGuardia, sir. Cadet, there are nuclear-armed B-1 bombers
leaving every hour on the hour from Dyess Air Force Base in
Texas, Ellsworth Air Force Base in South Dakota, Grand Forks
Air Force Base in North Dakota, McConnell Air Force Base in
Kansas, and Whiteman Air Force Base in Missouri. I want
you out of here and on one of them by 0800 hours—do you
comprehend the English language, cadet? Sir, yes, sir. Then why
are you still standing here? Sir, a crazy thing happened last

night, sir! What kind of crazy thing, cadet? Sir, we were getting
ready to go to a party and while I was waiting for Arleen
to finish getting dressed I was reading a John Donne poem
entitled "Love's Diet," which opens with the lines, "To what a
combersome unwieldiness / And burdenous corpulence my love
had growne." So Arleen was finally ready, and I put the book
down and we left the house, and we got in the car and took the
Holland Tunnel into Manhattan, and we're driving up Sixth
Avenue looking for a space, and plastered to a wall is a series of
posters advertising a band that's playing somewhere and what
do you think the band is called? Big Fat Love! I couldn't
believe it ... the eerie synchronicity, sir!

saliva of the fittest

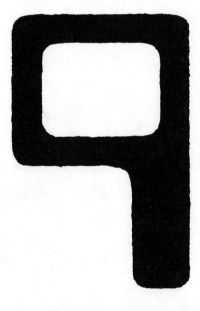

had a boyfriend who was a computer
nerd at Rensselaer Polytechnic

Institute and he would softly strum his steel guitar and sing
that the goddess of insurance dropped a feathery Nerf ball on
Isaac Newton's head, causing him to invent calculus so that
actuaries could calculate annuity premiums and he would
strongly suggest that the Incas built a 750-unit parking garage
for alien spacecraft in Machu Picchu and I would lay my head
on his thigh as big juicy soft dark-purple Soviet submarines
clustered in the bay for torpedo-loading practice. A hunting
accident left me with a 19-inch quadrangular cavity that
completely perforates my torso—I can stand directly in front of
your television set without obstructing the picture.... You can
see the skeleton of a giant waterbug and you can see the
skeleton of a giant entomologist. When I whipped him gently
with my sash, he made me say the cathected words. The
cathected words! he'd beg. Hertz, I'd whisper with the first
stroke. Oooooh, he'd say. Paine Webber. Oooooh! Deutsche Bank,

Reebok, Pennzoil, Taco Bell. And in the late afternoon sun, the trellised balcony would throw a grid of shadow across his acne-covered hunchback. They had warned tenants in high-rise buildings to expect some swaying, but we were unprepared for the severity.... Our building lurched from side to side like a metronome.

The hood of my Hyundai is dappled with the morning dew. A diagonal smear of chocolate across my windshield is the result of a malicious doughnut tossed from a trestle. A succession of nose jobs has left me with little more than a pinched piece of foreskin in the center of my face. I had a friend who had a friend who knew the manager of the Vegeta-belles, three comatose girls in antebellum organdy ball gowns who traveled the sideshow circuit on hospital gurneys...he had his own act in which he'd stand on a platform 15 feet above his curvaceous assistant who'd hold a doughnut outstretched and he'd urinate through the doughnut with such precision that not a single drop would splatter onto its circumference and he'd invite a member of the audience to come onstage, taste the doughnut, and prove it. And somehow this guy got us four ringside seats for the world lightweight championship fight, a bout that had been much ballyhooed because the antagonists were vicious men who genuinely loathed each other. The fight surpassed our expectations. Both boxers endured and meted out brutal, ruthless punishment and when the final bell rang at the end of the fifteenth round and their handlers had cut their gloves from their hands, they went at each other again with their bare fists and had to be restrained finally by a phalanx of celebrity fighters at ringside who, doffing their tuxedo jackets, leapt into the ring and, wielding their own gold-ringed fists, beat the 126-lb. competitors until they agreed to comport themselves with the dignity that befits a sport that dates back to 3,000 B.C. when, as depicted on cuneiform tablets recently unearthed near Reno, triumphant pugilists epoxied chunks of chipmunk meat to the huge "pizza of the pharaoh."

But a couple of days later there was a terrible terrible

accident. My friend was driving with his friend and his friend's friend and their car went off a bridge and plummeted into the bay. Police dragged the bay and pulled a car up. I recognized it immediately—the partially decomposed bodies of my three compatriots were still seated in the '69 Oldsmobile. It was an old car but they'd had it customized with a high-efficiency engine using cryogenic liquid propellants and also two strap-on solid-fuel boosters. Can I get in with them for a minute? I asked. I slid next to my pal in the front seat, his hands were still holding the steering wheel, there was seaweed all over him. My pal in the passenger seat was also frozen in position— switching radio stations. Owiginally we thought death was caused by pawalytic shellfish toxin, said the forensic pathologist, kills in half a second—death and wigor mortis are simultaneous—but we wuled that out. The forensic pathologist was only four. He was an astounding prodigy, the youngest forensic pathologist ever, but he had trouble pronouncing his Rs. Did you know that this car once belonged to Lyndon Lawouche, many owners ago? I shook my head at the little genius.

   That night Arleen and I got dressed rather nicely to have dinner with friends at a local restaurant. As we stepped out of the house and began walking towards the restaurant, I said to Arleen in a very solicitous tone of voice: You have a tiny bit of diarrhea right at the corner of your mouth. Arleen got very angry with me. Why do you have to say things like that? she said. She said that my humor was very hostile. Later she asked: Why do you have to be so cynical? I tried to explain that I was simply poking fun at the way couples groom each other en route to social events, but she still seemed hurt by the remark.
   A flying wing with no fuselage tows a face across the sky. The face in the sky has freckles and an oily forehead and braces and expels spearmint breath and tells me the most violent stories in a cracking pubescent voice...and then poking through the clouds comes the nose with blackheads! Now the flow of cerebrospinal fluid from my skull to my spinal column is like

the flow of ketchup from a bottle, moving slowly slowly and then in a great surge. At dawn we arrive at my sister's home in Las Vegas and the first thing I notice when we get inside is that all the silverware is bent, as if Uri Geller has been there. She has a stunning place—she's got a huge backyard with a driving range, archery, bumper cars, batting cages, video arcade, pizza, fried chicken, Ping Pong, saltwater pool, and a 120-foot diamond-vision stadium television screen which is showing the end of *All the President's Men*. Bruce Lee has just dealt the coup de grace to Nixon who lies supine on his front yard, neck broken, brain dead, incongruous tractor trailers passing on a nearby highway. After half a dozen superfluous punches, Bruce Lee collapses across his nemesis's insensate body, prostrate with what resembles postcoital exhaustion, hyperventilating until the police and his girlfriend Sondra arrive simultaneously with the apparent purpose of taking him away—to where . . . one can barely guess. A film is a spooled fuse. . . . Beyond its final frame, flickering emulsion and perforated tags, it explodes into an infinite number of indeterminate trajectories. But Sondra has brought a tiny LCD pocket television set so that Bruce Lee can watch the big football game. And while she kneels beside him, kissing his superficial but nonetheless sanguinary wounds, the policemen become engrossed with the game because the heavily favored team's quarterback, chased out of the pocket by blitzing linebackers, has just thrown an errant pass that's been picked off by a defensive back who, unmolested, runs it back 60 yards for a touchdown—the clock's run out—and the home team has won, pulling off a stunning upset. This play is shown over and over and over and over and over and over again, in slow motion, fast motion, isolated camera, pixilated camera, thermographic camera, and finally X-ray vision which shows leaping skeletons in a bluish void surrounded by 75,000 roaring skulls. And while the police sit like Druids in a circle on the ground, their attention riveted to the tiny TV, Bruce Lee and his girlfriend Sondra get up and walk quietly into the distance. . . .

■　■　■

—Scotch?

—Thanks.

—The thing of it is...the thing of it is... (He finishes pouring drink and hands it to Sondra.)...is that you don't know what a shoddy, loathsome, malignant person I really am ...because I don't even know yet, I'm just beginning to learn, you see.

—Well, I do know to a certain extent...For instance I know that since your father died you've been managing his estate and I know that you've been less than honest with your mother about certain financial details and that you've been terribly stingy with her when she's asked for a piddling little extra here and there.

—Yes, quite right. Another Scotch? You really tossed that one down.

—Yes, I think I'll have another one....Join me?

—Yes, I could use another myself. (He pours two large Scotches over ice, hands one to Sondra, and takes a long sip from his.) Yes, quite right.

—One could, I suppose, go as far as to say that you're swindling your own mother.

—But apparently it doesn't offend your sense of propriety enough for you to stop wanting to see me.

—I fancy you, Bruce.

—Sondra, would you like to watch a movie called *Nabonga* with Buster Crabbe?

—Actually I could use a bit more Scotch.

—Let me freshen these up. (He refills both glasses.) By the way, how do you like this Scotch?...I think it's special.

—Bruce, I don't know how to say this without sounding a bit precious...but when I drink this sort of very special Scotch, I feel like I've been placed in the bipolar field of the sacred and the profane, the licit and the illicit, the religious and the blasphemous....I feel as if six tungsten carbide blocks have converged on my brain from six directions, compacting it into a dense and perfect cube....Bruce, why don't we take these out onto the patio, it's a terribly lovely evening.

And as she steps out onto the patio, her Valkyrian bosom undulating with each step like a viscous liquid, a pterodactyl swoops down from the sky, snatches her in its beak, flies her to its nest, and drops her into the shrieking rictus of its offspring.

psychotechnologies of

the somber workaholics

i presume that you're there   the weight of your invisible
body straining the leather seat of my director's chair   that
strange fart wafting past me like the mildew of old
books   inhaled cigarette smoke assuming the shape of a
trachea and two lungs   you are a vivid impasto of vanishing
cream   you are the negative aggregate of a lifetime's
ablations   this is you after your gastrectomy and your
laryngectomy and pancreatectomy and craniectomy   but
chérie, you insult me by offering to buy me a drink in my own
home—drinks here are gratis and i do the offering   what's
more, you have the audacity to try and pick me up while my
wife is asleep in our connubial bed not fifteen yards from
here!   such bold incorporeal lust!   most american men
want to fuck something hairy—either a vagina or an asshole,
but all you offer is a circle—a bald circumference   well,
maybe i will, just to keep the night alive   go ahead, muse,
bend over and tell me i'm the greatest thing

after being chased across the pampa all day by a bola-swinging
centaur with wine cooler on his breath and sodomy in his
eyes...

the doorbell rings...
—hello, we're selling ourselves to raise money for the
    gestapo   we're like peppers—we come in two colors, red
    and green   if you buy one of us, me for example, you can
    bring me as your date to the gestapo club and then when you
    take me home you can split me open and lay me out across a
    hot cheese steak and eat me
—what if i want to buy both of you, i asked
—*tant mieux*, said the cop-cum-pepper, gently drawing the tip
    of his nightstick across his partner's crisscrossed bandoliers of
    bullets and tranquilizer darts
—well, i still don't understand...what are you?   are you like
    transsexuals or what?   i don't get it
—no, man, essentially we're cops, but we were bred to be like
    peppers   it's like we're hybrids mengele developed in his
    garden in paraguay   so we're cops, we're gestapo—but
    essentially you can eat us   and if you open us up, we're
    essentially like peppers—fleshy-walled, many-seeded, etc. etc.
    etc.

thick white smoke billows from the factory smokestack
and forms an undulating somatic shape
but, like a sung dynasty poet, i am too drunk to
assume gigantic proportions and embrace the industrial genie,
too drunk to lick the white soot from her big molecules with my
tongue

i'm playing with a hair in my ear—and i tug the hair and
there's a very strange, slightly painful sensation deep in my
head, followed by a flood of memories—the hair turns out to be
connected to the mnemonic section of the brain (the

hippocampus)—it's like pulling chatty cathy's string—instead
of talk though, memories ensue:
     shaving cream gurgles up from a plaster of paris volcano
     in miss cosgrove's social studies class

oh man, i wanted to kiss the harsh authoritarian words of miss
cosgrove
i wanted to find the source of her voice with my tongue
i wanted to strum the taut, cold, acrid strings of her vocal cords
with my tongue
but like you, su tung-p'o, i was too drunk

jill is teaching tess how to speak in a flat tone of voice
you have to sound like this, jill says flatly
jill, i just can't speak with that flat affect! says tess
with fierce gesticulation, her voice cresting with emotion

male hormone oozes from every fucking pore in my body   i
sweat male hormone   i drool male hormone   my tears are
pure male hormone   when i exert myself i stink of
testosterone   my balls are like giant planets engulfed in
chaotic storms of toxic gases   i'm like some beast who marks
off his territory with his reeking yellow urine   my sperm
is like a virulent milkshake of recombinant worms   my
penis smells like an uncorked decanter of fermented
smegma   geysers of purple molten shit explode from my
asshole, destroying villages in its path   i'm all man   100%
man

there's a bar on the highway which caters almost exclusively to
authority figures and the only drink it serves is lite beer and
the only food it serves is surf and turf and one night the place
is filled with cops and state troopers and gym teachers and

green berets and toll attendants and game wardens and crossing guards and umpires

each man loves his wife so very much   sometimes he hugs her with such ardor that it leaves her gasping for breath   he feels as if he wants to literally get inside her skin with her, to draw her flesh over them both as if it were a sheet or a quilt, to feel the palpitations and quivers of her internal organs warm and slick with their secretions against his nakedness   when she eats, he puts his ear to her cheek as she chews to better savor the music of her mandibles   he puts an ear to her stomach and enjoys the churning and gurgles of her digestion and an ear to her lower abdomen to note the sibilant rush of gas as it winds through her intestines, to the small of her back to hear each crack of her vertebrae, between her shoulder blades for the soft expansion and contraction of her lungs   at night, while she sleeps, he puts his ear against her scalp and listens for the almost inaudible rustling of her hair as it grows

in the old days they'd just throw you in a big iron caldron and boil you   now they put you in a teflon no-stick saucepan and they sauté you for a while in walnut oil   i knew one guy who was poached   i know one guy who was fricaseed   i know one guy who was diced benihana style and stir-fried   i knew one guy—he was only in the steamer for three minutes and they said, take him out we'll eat him al dente   and they give these people varsity letters   my father took me to an endocrinologist and the endocrinologist said, he'll always be *eine kleine mensch,* don't send him to no state school 'cause see he's bite-size … he'll make a perfect hors d'oeuvre   that night my mother came up to my bedroom and she said, if you ever see one of them in a letter sweater or letter jacket you run as fast as you can unless you wanna end up with a frilly toothpick through your back or unless you wanna end up between two slices of wonder bread 'cause ain't no deus ex machina gonna

swoop through the skylight and save your white ass   i never
suspected you though, baby   you were so nice to me   i
took you back to your apartment   you poured me a nice cold
heineken   i said, baby, i've been lonely for too long   i got
six years of pent-up rhapsodies in me   then i saw that fuckin'
varsity ankle bracelet   i said, uh-uh, no way, and i tried to
escape but you squirted me with bug spray and my legs went
numb

the next thing i know i'm in the emergency room at the hospital
and the doctor looks at me and says, "mah man, you
dead"   he says, "i gotta help get your soul out of your body
but it's gonna cost you a little extra"   "feel around in my
pocket," says my eerie disembodied voice, "you can take my visa
card"   "i'm gonna have to squeeze the soul out of your body
by rolling you up like a tube of toothpaste..."

now, i am the sound of a playing card
ticking the spokes of a bicycle wheel

that is not a sky, it is a grid   it is a grid of thin black lines
superimposed over a bleached ceiling   the stars and planets
and moons and satellites are bleached out   the constellations
which once seemed indelible have been expunged by sweaty
grim-faced charwomen who came to the beach at night with
scouring pads and long poles   the logos, graffiti, toponyms,
and exhortations to "love and be loved" were soon replaced by
the glaucous swaths of industrial stripping machines   the
technicians did not polish the sky with their lamb's wool pads
because the artists and designers had decided that the sky
would be more beautiful and more numinous with a matte
finish as opposed to a high sheen   and when the black grid
was installed even the most mawkish elegiac poets could not
mourn the demise of the old sky because the black grid which
stretched endlessly in all directions was so unspeakably lovely,

because language was made superfluous by the black grid's
perfect representation of the godliness of the human
imagination   today, beneath the black grid, teenagers disport
themselves on the beach   they move with one will from their
blankets to the surf and then, as if motivated by a single
atavistic instinct, they move back to their blankets   en masse
they eat hot dogs   and then suddenly en masse they drink
pepsi   and when nightfall comes and the lymphatic teenagers
(the gawky, squat, sinewy, and nubile) fall asleep en masse and
their tucked recumbent bodies litter the beach, it is perfectly
quiet and perfectly dark except, suddenly, for the white
headlights of a sports car careening down the corniche

when i first met trudy she was wearing a t-shirt that said
SMITH COLLEGE SQUASH TEAM   i asked her if she went
to smith   yeah, she said   are you on the squash
team?   yeah, but i hang out with a bunch of animals, she
said, pointing to a group of clean-cut all-american kids in
turtleneck sweaters and white loafers sitting on a three-foot-
high chocolate-covered vanilla ice cream bar in the shape of a
valentine's day heart

the hippopotamus feeds on soft vegetation,
his excrement feeds the fish,
his pajamas dance convulsively from the clothesline

the sperm whale feeds on cuttlefish
and secretes ambergris to protect his intestines from the sharp
bones,
his silk negligee is whipped by the wind

the swordsmith hammers a sandwich of iron and steel
and gives it a bath of fire and water,
his wife is 19 inches diagonally

turkish women abhor body hair

hello, mark   this is elizabeth hurlick   i'm one of trudy's
friends from school   trudy asked me to call and tell you that
when she gets home from work she's going to want to make love
tout de suite and then eat 'cause she's got an early squash
practice so she wants you to season the chicken with some basil
and oregano and garlic and onion powder and paprika and put
it in the oven at about 350° and then she wants you to run a hot
bath and add some of the bayberry rum and spice bath beads
which she says are in a silver crabtree and evelyn tin on the
blue shelf next to the hair dryer and q-tips and she wants you
to soak in the tub for a while   she says there's already a
washcloth in there or you can use her loofah   and she said
that while you're in the tub you should masturbate almost to the
point of orgasm and stop and that way you'll have a more
copious ejaculation later when you have sex with trudy because
trudy says you have to propitiate the squash god and she says
that the squash god is in the mood for a really super-copious
ejaculation   and she said to tell you that when you get out of
the tub you can daub some of your chanel pour homme cologne
on your chest and in the hair on your belly and near your navel
but she doesn't want you to use any deodorant under your arms
because when you're having sex she wants your armpits to smell
kind of macho sort of raunchy kind of ruggedly homo sapien
kind of rural   and she wants you to wait for her wearing
either the red or the white-and-gold kimono danny and kristen
brought you from japan, whichever one you prefer   and you
should wait by the window in the study, sort of voluptuously
languidly posed like oscar wilde in the photograph by sarony,
she said you'll know which one she means—it's in the
montgomery hyde biography—and when she comes in through
the door she wants you to say, i'm extremely utterly enervated
from having spent all afternoon watching sparrows caper about
the fire escape   and then you should nonchalantly let your
kimono fall open so your meat sort of pokes out   and then
she wants you to lift her skirt up and take her underpants
off and she wants you to rub your knuckles up and down
her perineum   if you're writing this down that's spelled

p-e-r-i-n-e-u-m   it's the area between her anus and her
genitals   and she said to tell you that while you're fucking
you should try to keep an eye on the clock so the chicken
doesn't burn   i hope you don't mind me leaving this sort of
intimate personal message on your answering machine   but
i'm a really really good friend of trudy's and trudy's told me all
about you and i hope we can all get together sometime maybe
for burritos and a video on the vcr or something   trudy says
you're creepy in a sort of attractive way and that sounds fun

yoo hoo! buzz called out. y'all got any crème de cacao?

Yoo-hoo! Buzz called out. Y'all got any crème de cacao?

Muriel, skinny, sweating, fanning herself with a copy of *The Protocols of the Elders of Zion,* observed Buzz through the screen door. Come inside, Buzz, she said, it's too hot to holler. She was wearing a pair of faded madras shorts and one of her father's white button-down shirts—its tails knotted just above her navel, her bare midriff a taut circumference of translucent flesh glazed with perspiration. If you came to murder me, you're too late—I'm already dead from heat prostration.

Buzz loped in, doffed his baseball cap, stanched his wet brow with a sleeve, replaced the cap on his head, and grinned at Muriel.

But Grandma told Buzz to leave the room. When Grandma told Buzz to leave the room he fell to the floor and kissed her feet, begging her to let him stay. Buzz, you'd slobber over an old woman's varicose veins just so she'd let you stay in the room, wouldn't you? Grandma asked contemptuously.

Yes, Buzz whimpered.

Grandma rolled up a magazine and hit Buzz on the side of the head.... Buzz's mask was knocked loose. There was no skin beneath that mask. There were two white eyeballs protruding on stems from a mass of oozing blood-red musculature.

Grandma smoothed her hair back with spit and the palm of her hand. Honey, she said to me, go to my vanity table and fetch me my jar of cold cream and catfish slime.... I'm old, children, my wooden leg's sequoia and you can count its rings. Child, she said to Muriel, fetch the *TV Guide* and read me what's on.

Muriel got the *TV Guide*, flipped to Tuesday 8 P.M., and read aloud: "The Making of Jeanne d'Arc II" chronicles the abortive attempt by a pair of Israeli sleaze merchants to produce a sequel to the 1431 original which catapulted the amenorrheic daughter of a Domrémy farmer into international superstardom.

Nah, said Grandma, I think I've seen that one.

Muriel read on: "Daddy Promised Us Salami and Eggs, the Cunning Pragmatist"—a guy who's out one day innocently having a chicken chimichanga all by himself at a restaurant politely excuses himself from the table and goes to the men's room and someone sidles up to him at the urinal and injects him in the right buttock with a powerful designer drug that leaves him cataleptic but fully sentient and sells him for $100,000 to the Museum of Natural History where he's dressed as a Netsilik Eskimo and imprisoned in a glass-encased exhibit with a paraffin Netsilik woman and six paraffin huskies who are harnessed to a low-rider sled with hydraulic runners and a scrimshaw steering wheel and to ensure that he does not waste away, he's given intravenous nutrients every night by a horrible man with rotten teeth who reeks of cheap schnapps, and his son and his daughter-in-law do absolutely nothing to notify either the police or the media, which confirms his original suspicion that they are accessories to his abduction and partook of a portion of the $100,000, and the greedy amoral bastards have the temerity to bring his sweet grandson Douglas to the museum to gawk and gesticulate at him—starring Brian Keith, Buddy Ebsen, Nipsey Russell, and Lesley Ann Warren.

Nah, said Grandma, what else is on?

There's a show called "A Tumult of Pubic Hair and Bobbing Flaccid Penises as Sweaty Naked Chubby Men Run from the Sauna Screaming: Snake! Snake!"

What's that about?

It's pretty much like the title says—there's a snake in a sauna and it scares a group of chubby men who run naked and screaming and they show a lot of pubic hair and bobbing penises that are really really flaccid.

And who's in it?

It also stars Brian Keith, Buddy Ebsen, Nipsey Russell, and Lesley Ann Warren.

Nah, said Grandma, I'm just gonna go up and hit the sack. Child, send Buzz up to read me my bedtime story.

By the time Buzz got upstairs to Grandma's bedroom she was already under the covers.

Buzz, she said, fetch me my bedtime book.

Buzz went to the bookcase and fetched Grandma's beautiful leather-bound edition of *Nocturnal Narratives for Retirees*.

What would you like to hear tonight, Grandma?

I'd like to hear "The Medicine-Chest Killers."

Buzz scanned the table of contents, flipped to the appropriate page, cleared his throat, and began: "The deformation bomb was the most insidious bomb ever developed by the Pentagon. It was a bomb that changed the shape of things. A bomb that warped the line. A bomb that corrugated the smooth. Its impact coursed across the land like the wind which row by row bends the field of ripe corn and it gnarls and buckles every shape in its path and it does not distinguish between the animate and the inanimate. Two men known as the medicine-chest killers were riding in a car. They saw the flash. They heard its dampened pop. They saw the wave of distortion sweep towards them like the wind which row by row bends the field of ripe corn. They felt it pass over their car. Laughing roguishly, they drove on—their car misshapen and pleated, their spines wildly zigzagged, their fingers veering off at the knuckles in a welter of oblique angles, their cigarettes dangling from their lips like smoldering corkscrews. They arrived at an isolated farmhouse. They snuck upstairs. As usual, they headed straight for the medicine chest and they popped all the pills: the Excedrin, the estrogen, Pamprin, Percodan, Ex-Lax, Zantac, they knocked back the last two tetracyclines with swigs of Halley's M.O. Downstairs they tied their victims' hands behind their backs with dental floss, they blindfolded them with surgical gauze..."

Just skip to the end, boy, I'm too sleepy to follow that plot, Grandma interrupted groggily.

Buzz flipped to the final page: "And the one thousand begin entering heaven: Ozzy Osbourne, Cynthia Ozick, Tommy John, etc. etc., each with the solitary clang of a coin falling into an empty bank."

Buzz glanced over the book towards Grandma. Sure enough, she was fast asleep. He quietly returned the volume to the bookshelf, turned off the light, and tiptoed out of the room.

He went downstairs, he put his mask back over his hideous face, and he went to see if Muriel had found any crème de cacao.

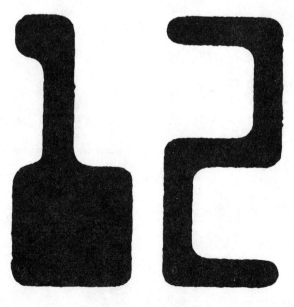

**I** was doing curls with a barbell and I became so sweaty and muscular that I couldn't stop fondling myself and thinking to myself, What a little savage you're becoming, and I ran into the kitchen to get the olive oil because I wanted to coat myself with it and somewhere in the back of my mind I wanted to be blinded and then pull the pillars of the temple down ... and you were sleeping ... and I remember lying down next to you and the almost inaudible splash of a gnat diving into the pool of perspiration that had formed in my navel must have frightened you because you jumped up in the bed and began screaming something about how two of America's most beloved screen stars, Hume Cronyn and Jessica Tandy, had been killed in a tragic accident. While filming Dino de Laurentiis's production of T. S. Eliot's "The Love Song of J. Alfred Prufrock," directed by John Landis who's known for his spectacular special effects, the huge metal robotic women who come and go talking of Michelangelo collapsed—crushing the aging Oscar winners.

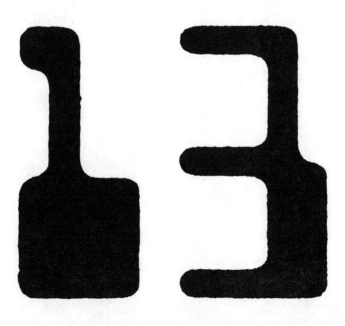

gather the 10,000 americans in irreversible comas and book
    them into rooms at the sheraton center in midtown
when clouds in the night sky resemble the x-ray of christ's
    cheekbone shattered by the split-fingered fastball of the
    devil
the exact date of the atomic armageddon will be written in the
    cursive script of hairs on a bar of soap
and each smirking bellhop will be a baby elvis
and hot urine will cascade down the sides of sugar mountain
if you find one of my eyelashes on the street, please return it to
    me ... or one of the hairs from my legs—please—take it to
    a police station, there's a reward   particularly the right
    leg, the leg that used to kick field goals for pocahontas
    high in mahwah   don't you remember?   our silly
    adolescent pact   we each pledged to eat whichever one
    of us died first   we didn't even know the meaning of the
    word *necrophagia* then   we were just real american kids

with real american ids   ever since then i've been
swallowing garlic capsules and giving myself daily
injections of basil and oregano so that i'll be properly
seasoned for you   each shred of dead skin that i peel
from my neck and deposit furtively into an ashtray at a
cocktail party is a metonymic précis of my severe
instability

do you know me?   my american express card says simply:
perishable vertebrate—don't fuck after date stamped on
bottom

i had fifteen fatal diseases induced by pesticides, exhaust fumes,
cosmetics, charcoal-broiled and fatty foods and they were
all cured instantly by a sugar-coated placebo called a milk
dud, but then they recrudesced exponentially so that i had
225 mortal illnesses   my doctor painted a grim picture
of each disease   he did my leukemia in acrylic on
canvas, he did my mercury poisoning in watercolor
on composition board, my asbestosis in day-glo enamel
on wood, and my emphysema in synthetic polymer
on plexiglas   a listener called in to say that my
broadcast signals were becoming weaker and weaker   i
said, i'm still on the air despite 225 diseases, but i decided
to go up to the roof and examine the colinear beam
antenna   when the elevator got stuck, a woman in a
taupe leather blazer and suede necktie kissed me, she let
me put my hand in her shirt and feel her breasts, she let
me put my hand down her trousers and hold her hard-on,
she said: i'm the angel of death   where've you been all
my life? i asked, flushed with love at first sight   i've been
compiling a dossier on your psychopathology, she said, as
the elevator launched through the roof and exploded in
midair like the space shuttle *challenger*   we checked
into a montmartre hotel frequented by thieves, prostitutes,
and drug addicts but the room didn't have a television set
so we checked out   in palermo, we installed ourselves at
the grand albergo e delle palme, where wagner had written
much of *parsifal*—our room had a 25-inch color TV with

random access remote control   i took a milk dud and
felt increasingly spiritualized, dematerialized... i felt an
abrupt separation from my body   i traveled through
a dark tunnel, over a field of glockenspiels and pom-
poms   i sang the song of the extremely subtle energy-
wind-mind   i slept in a sandwich, enveloped in sheets of
fatty smoked meats   on the 6 o'clock news the police
commissioner was issuing a statement concerning a woman
who'd detonated her libido in a bowling alley, injuring two
off-duty cops: "officers russo and mendoza of the 3rd
precinct were engaged in off-duty recreational activities at
the roosevelt bowling lanes when at approximately 1500
hours an explosion occurred   immediately subsequent to
the explosion, russo and mendoza observed the suspect—a
caucasian female approximately 18 to 20 years of age—
levitating above the lanes, discharging a powerful libidinal
bioluminescence   officer russo and officer mendoza, as a
result of exposure to heavy doses of the suspect's
radioactive libido, have regressed to the anal-sadistic stage
and are presently barricaded inside the bowling alley
where they are whining and manipulating their bowel
movements"   i turned the television off, got dressed,
and we had dinner with a group of moderate iranians
in the blazing headlights of an oncoming subway car, my
      mother's skin is as translucent as the tissue-thin page of a
      norton anthology
my flesh is completely transparent; in 1956 i sat on a bridge
      chair in the middle of a rodeo and let elizabeth taylor
      watch my heart pump purple blood through my aorta and
      the mucous membrane of my stomach secrete gastric juice
      and my vasa deferentia carry sperm from the testes and i
      said: i hope you're not turned off by the
      verfremdungseffekt of my transparent body
my exquisite epic and lyric verse have been featured in
      magazines across the country
grateful acknowledgment is made to the following publications
      in which some of these poems first appeared: *good*

housekeeping for "have you ever felt the cold dick of your own shadow? (prelude to a quaalude)"; *McCall's* for "shall i compare thee to loan sharking, gambling, hijacking, extortion, union racketeering, cigarette smuggling, home video pornography, or narcotics?"; *cosmopolitan* for "have you ever been hit in the head by a cruise missile?"; and *ladies' home journal* for "have you ever been lying on your back under a viaduct in a tranquil rural area with a blade of grass in your mouth and suddenly you look up as a tractor trailer veers off the road and crashes through the guardrail above and it's plummeting straight down at you and you only have time to catch its license plate 'new hampshire—live free or die' before its two and a half tons crush your helpless body?"

these spicy, violent, superbly plotted verses are perfect for television
        across the tundra snow did fall
        flecked with blue like fab and all

my father slapped me across the face with his hairy knuckles and his fraternity ring and he said, tell the horrible story!   tell it!   and the earth shook because of the earthquake near cleveland and the drag strip was busy.... you couldn't help but stop and listen   even in the newsroom every once in a while the typewriters would stop   there was one drag race after another   the caterwaul of two engines   did you ever put your ear right up against someone's fly when he unzips his trousers— that's what it was like   the obbligato of screaming engines, of berserk motors   also against that background you could hear the sound of teenagers opening their cans of coke—that simultaneous pop and sibilance   throughout the night this special sound occurred   it was incessant, but exhibited no discernable pattern   my father took a sloppy swig of chowder from his thermos and spit a diced clam onto the table   i'll let you off this time, he said to it and dispatched it with a fillip into the starry starry night   tell the horrible

story! he said to me, brandishing his chapped fist   oh
god, he said, coughing up blood and sputum   don't tell
it, he said, sing it to me, son   sing it—you have your
grandmother's sweet irish tenor, son—sing it   i was
going to tell the story about the time my mother kicked me
down the steps and she was standing back at the top
looking down at me—she was in her black bra and
panties—and she said . . .   i said sing it, son!   sing
it!!

my mother kicked me down the steps
she was standing at the top
in her black bra and panties
laughing shrilly
etc.

this father is smoothing his hair. . . . he is making half a dozen
      psychodramatic gestures like tackling the son and giving
      him a kung fu chop to the throat   this father's nose is so
      big that it blocks the sunlight, hindering the
      photosynthesis of green plants and leading to the
      breakdown of vital food chains

this father's nose is so big that if you took each of his nose hairs,
      tied them together, and put a hook on the end, you could
      stand on the moon and fish in lake michigan

in the pitch-darkness, i could hear the sound of grandma's
      guitar   in the early mesozoic era, grandma played a
      slide guitar solo that lasted for eight years, causing the
      universal landmass to break up into continents

grandma, you are the primordial monster   you are the
      monster who predates chronology   when the big bang
      was heard, you were already a fearless businesswoman,
      throwing back your head and laughing yes! to all of life's
      challenges   you are grandma, the great bulimic
      divinity, who roams the moors with a flamethrower and a
      spray gun filled with barbecue sauce and when you see a
      lamb you douse it with sauce and you say stand back! and
      you charbroil it with your flamethrower and then when
      you've eaten an entire barbecued lamb you go behind a

bush and stick your finger down your throat—and you
leave a business card in the jawbone of each carcass that
reads: you've been ritually sacrificed, bolted down, and
barfed up by granny—america's preeminent flesh-eating
deity
grandma, help me sing—help me sing of the nude gladiators
who are tan except for white buttocks, who flex their glutei
maximi in unison   help me sing of grandpa who went to
the store for a tube of toothpaste 16,000 lines of dactylic
hexameter ago and never returned
some people say that grandpa lives in the bekáa valley and that
all he has in his cupboard is a swollen can of vichyssoise
and a container of nondairy creamer; some people say that
he's become a human ashtray to a gang of sadistic girls
who hold court in a lavish trump tower apartment; and
some people say that he's fallen in love with a pink rose in
his garden—they say that each night he creeps out in the
dew, wearing an expensive ribbed scented condom made
from a sheep's intestine—and he bicycles to the center of
his maze where his pink rose lives—and he gently bends
its long stem and he cradles the rose in his arms and kisses
its petals, mumbling—and he snorts the yellow powdery
pollen from its stamens... as bees stand on the sidelines
waving hi mom!
the rain is intermixed with tickertape
the desolate plain is littered with costumes of the commedia
dell'arte doffed in great panic
from a lone mesa in the distance comes the numinous voice of
my grandma, the grandma of all men: you with the tiny
degenerate eyes, the $200 loafers, the mohair suit, and fat
gold pinky ring, compulsively massaging skin moisturizer
into your hands—you are the only grandson who does not
flee in terror
i am estranged from most men   my american express card
says simply: multicellular animal with specialized
digestive cavities—requires corrective glasses

will you purge my mortal grossness so
that i shall like an airy spirit go,
  i mumbled, writhing like a stripper from chippendale's
a guitar chord of incalculable decibels is strummed, rending the
  earth between my feet
grandma, speak to me
you speak me, she says.... and with these words my own larynx
  resonates
grandma, take me in your arms
these are my arms, she says.... and i feel my own elbows ache
  with rheumatism
grandma, let me sleep in your womb
this is your womb, she says.... and my testicles inflate like two
  balloons and my penis unfurls into the air like a paper
  noisemaker
now sing of the nude gladiators who are tan except for white
  buttocks and if anyone tries to stop you, remember, not
  only do you sing under the auspices of grandma, the
  primordial bulimic monster who predates chronology and
  flame-broils sheep, but your singing is also supported by
  logistical elements from the army's xviii airborne corps,
  marine attack planes, and naval gunfire from the
  battleship *new jersey*   i have spoken
there is total darkness   there is a flourish of horns   there is
  light   three beach towels   blackout   pause
  lights up   three nude gladiators on beach towels
  tan except for white buttocks   scars from whips, lion
  bites, spiked balls, and chariot wheel blades   nude
  gladiators flex glutei maximi in unison   flex relax   flex
  relax   flex relax   pause   three phones ring   nude
  gladiators slowly crane necks over left shoulders to survey
  audience and then reach for phones upstage with
  right hands as if making synchronized swimming strokes
  hello, say NGs in unison   voice of telephone interlocutor
  (audible to audience): moaning   NGs: who?
  voice: more moaning   nude gladiators take receivers

from ears, hold aloft, and then smash down into
phone cradles   blackout   pause   lights up
receivers held aloft   blackout   sound of receivers
being smashed down   pause   voice: i do not
need your primitive telecommunication devices to make
myself audible   lights up   nude gladiators have
scrambled to their knees in obeisance, bowing up and
down and up and down   NGs (scared, awed): identify
yourself   voice: flood of exquisite lyric verse   NGs: oh,
that was good, that was good   voice: did you like
that?   NGs: that was really good!   voice: can you
three guys work the grabber?   NGs: what's the
grabber?   voice: it's a special rescue crane   NGs:
standard or automatic?   voice: standard   NGs: we
could learn   voice: good, i'm sending you three to el
paso   blackout   pause   lights up   a woman is
on the ledge of a tall building, covering her armpits   a
policeman yells up to her through a bullhorn: no one's
going to arouse you!   woman: no te creo   los
conquistadores no vinieron sólo por oro!   policeman
hands bullhorn to priest   priest: isabel, me llamo
padre vallejo   absolutely nobody is going to kill
you softly with his song   you have my solemn word
of honor   policeman gets on squad car radio: get
the grabber over here now!   we'll try to stall her
voices of three nude gladiators: we'll be right there
blackout   lights up   three NGs are in grabber
cab operating controls   grabber pincers rise high in
air and pluck woman off ledge   woman is waving
arms hysterically: it tickles!   it itches!   qué músculos!
blackout
    when the lights come up again, the seminude gladiators are
driving to newark airport after learning that kim il sung
has been shot   they are wearing jeans designed by le
corbusier   they are displaying severe psychomotor
agitation, nihilistic delusions, and ego-syntonic
obsessions   i give them the minnesota multiphasic

personality inventory
what fruit can soothe the mind,
but mellaril?
what soup, but stelazine—
the intravenous broth that's just like grandma used to
make
the semi-NGs are exercising their first amendment rights
they are singing the song of the extremely subtle
energy-wind-mind   the singers are dead, they sing, the
singers are dead dead dead   wasn't it mallarmé who
said, "when a superhuman being shampoos its hair, it
thinks of death?"   in the sky, a thin crescent of cloud
punctuates the empty azure like a single comma   two of
the semi-NGs have prophylactics in the back pockets of
their tight jeans, one has a packet of duck sauce   there
goes the fuji blimp, says one   there's a redhead from
scarsdale in a saab, says the second   and what are you
reading? i ask the semi-NG with duck sauce in his
pocket   *of sinuses and nephews*   it's superb   did
you know that alexander the great's nephew had
degenerative sinusitis?   did you know that chuck yeager
was scheduled to fly the U-2 spy plane that the russians
shot down but he had to take his nephew to get his sinuses
drained so francis gary powers got the assignment instead?
a scented nuclear warhead manufactured by mcdonnell douglas
in collaboration with estée lauder passes overhead, leaving
in its wake a light, floral fragrance with a touch of citrus
and spice, and winds of 750 miles per hour   children tie
strings to their anvils and fly them in the supersonic
turbulence   and the yellow sheets of enuretic
adolescents are torn from their clotheslines and sail
through the air like magic carpets   and these magic
carpets bring me home, to the glory that was greece, and
the grandeur that was rome
a bongo-playing cuban bandleader fell on the field of battle
today   innovator, he had been the first to shoot with
three cameras in front of a live audience, succumbing to
lung cancer   in all the years since their divorce he

never maligned lucy caused by his unrepentant passion for strong cuban cigars   he was the only bongo-playing cuban bandleader in the history of broadcasting to succumb in front of a live audience caused by his unrepentant passion   after their divorce, lucy released a statement through her press secretary, saying: "i'll never marry another bongo-playing cuban bandleader... none could compare to him—he was the first to succumb to his unrepentant passion for my strong press secretary"   *sic transit gloria mundi*   foucault died of aids before he could finish the fourth volume of his history of sexuality   after he divorced lucy, he sold her his interest in their production company and with the exception of cameo appearances he retired from the history of broadcasting   pindar wrote: "... to all comes / the wave of death and falls unforeseen / even on him who foresees it / but honor grows for the dead / whose tender repute a god fosters"   so perhaps someday a schoolboy will stand before a class in the history of sexuality and recite these unforgettable words: "a bongo-playing cuban bandleader fell on the field of battle today / he was the first to shoot a live audience he never maligned"

the very thought of them

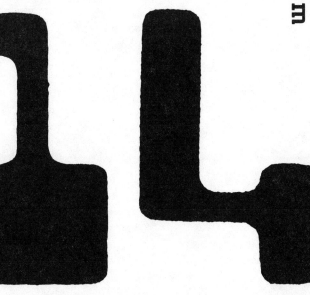

The office had been abuzz for the past couple of weeks over the news about Bob's new bride. And now excitement reached a more sustained pitch with the opportunity to finally meet Gloria (as we learned she was named) at an upcoming party being given to celebrate our completion of a large project we'd been working on for an Israeli film company. What we knew of the "Bob and Gloria Story" was extremely romantic and entrancing. They had fallen in love at first sight, there'd been a whirlwind courtship, and in the middle of dinner at an intimate little bistro, they'd decided to fly off to Vegas and get married at the Chapel of the Belles. The day before the party, talk around the office revolved around nothing else but speculation about Gloria and our shared happiness for Bob who all of us agreed was the nicest and most intelligent boss any of us had ever worked for. Well, that night I arrived at the party and immediately began scanning the living room for Bob and his new wife who'd presumably be by his side. I mingled a bit, snared some hors

d'oeuvres, had a drink or two. The apartment, a lovely but very
small one-bedroom affair, had become a bit stifling and I went
into the bedroom to deposit my sport coat. There was Bob
beaming from ear to ear and he embraced me warmly—I'd
never seen him looking so happy and serene. "So where is she?"
I asked. "I'm dying to meet the woman who put such a smile on
your face." Bob led me over to the bathroom. "She's in here
changing her sweater—she got a little hot out there—come take
a look," he whispered, opening the bathroom door a crack and
putting his finger to his lips to advise stealth. I quietly edged
over to the door and took a peek. I almost died. There was a
woman with the sunken, wrinkled face of an eighty- or ninety-
year-old. She had her shirt off and she was standing in front of
the mirror about to slip on a blouse. And this withered hag, this
apparent octogenarian, had the body of a male Olympic
swimmer. The long lean sinewy arms, the powerful V-shaped
upper torso, without a single ounce of extra fat anywhere, a
body that only comes after thousands of hours of laps and speed
training. I was flabbergasted—but before I could even react to
what I'd seen, Bob jabbed me in the ribs with his elbow. "And
you should taste her oatmeal!" he said, winking slyly.

Eventually we all met Gloria that night at the party and I
could tell from the expressions on my colleagues' faces that they
too were utterly confused at what they'd encountered. But our
deep deep respect and affection for Bob prevented us from
exchanging anything that could be construed as malicious
gossip or even mild consternation over this strange bride. And
in fact, when we returned to the office that Monday, and for
that entire week, no one said a word about it except to offer
some trite expression of happiness for Bob. We all felt so
strongly about what it meant to work for someone like Bob that
we were at a loss as to how to react to this situation. Bob was
the most innovative and effective production manager the
company had ever seen. He was an utterly fair man, a
magnanimous man, a compassionate man, a man who never
hesitated to go to bat for you with the muckety-mucks at the
top. That weekend, I got a call early Sunday morning—one of

the guys from the office, crying. "Gloria ... Bob's wife ... She's been killed." "Killed! How? ... My God, they were just married. ... How's Bob?" I asked, pulling my pants on. "He's taking it pretty hard." Over the next few hours, I managed to piece together what had actually happened. Apparently each night Gloria had been sneaking out of the house and roaming the countryside, raiding local farmers' chicken coops and killing and eating the chickens. And finally Saturday night, a farmer had heard a commotion in his henhouse, grabbed his shotgun, and killed Gloria in flagrante delicto. The funeral was Monday. The entire office staff was there in black suits and dresses, ashen-faced, grim, some weeping. Bob was standing by the open coffin. I walked over to pay my respects and offer whatever words of support that I could muster. I looked down into the coffin. Bob had instructed the mortician not to alter her appearance. There was the face of the shriveled old crone now pocked with heavy-gauge shot, wisps of feathers and shards of bone adhering to the coagulated chicken blood that ringed her mouth. She was wearing only a pair of striped men's briefs—the very very tight kind worn by athletes in swimming and diving competition. Her body, except for the gunshot wounds, could have been that of a male model in an ad for a health spa. Bob looked at me. His eyes were red from crying. Putting his arm around me, he looked back into the coffin. "I've never known a woman who loved life as much as she did," he said. Well, over the next few months we all watched Bob go through the long painful process of grieving and gradually putting his life back in order. That spring he bought a beautiful 40-foot pleasure boat and he named it the *Joie de Vivre* in honor of his late wife. And on Memorial Day weekend he invited a bunch of us out to the boat for a leisurely little cruise along the coast, fishing, relaxing, eating, and drinking. And as you might expect, there was a terrible terrible accident. . . .

in a black blur of nightsticks

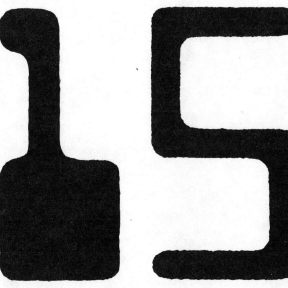

'm like so thrilled. You won't believe who's coming over. Geoffrey Tasner. He's like the greatest archer in the whole country! He won a gold medal in Seoul.... He's got endorsements from all the major archery equipment companies in the world. There's like a quiver named after him. And this really big apple company—I think it's Granny Smith or Golden Delicious—is supposed to use him in a commercial where he's like this William Tell guy who's standing on top of the World Trade Center and he shoots a Granny Smith or Golden Delicious apple off the Statue of Liberty's head with this laser beam crossbow.... Oh God, Mom, there's the doorbell! It's him! I gotta go. OK, Mom. OK... OK ...OK. OK. OK, Mom...gotta go. OK...OK...OK...OK. OK, Mom...OK. OK, I will...OK. OK. OK. OK. Gotta go, Mom. OK. OK...OK...OK. OK...OK, Mom. OK. OK. OK. OK, Mom. Gotta go...OK...OK...OK...OK. OK, Mom. OK... OK, I will. OK. OK. OK...OK, gotta go, Mom. OK. OK. OK. OK, bye.

—Geoffrey, how wonderful to see you!

—I get no thrill in seeing a constipated person take risks that people say are foolish, and yet get away with them.

—How true.... I get no thrill in seeing a constipated person take risks that people say are foolish, and yet get away with them, either. But Geoffrey, what's wrong? What's wrong, baby, you seem so distracted, so preoccupied. Was Seoul really weird? Did the Koreans fuck with your head? Tell me, baby. You can really talk to me.

—Dirty plates sometimes race through my head! Do you have any idea what that's like?

—Geoffrey, I want you to sit down right now and I want you to relax. Would you like a snack? I know from the *Sports Illustrated* article that you're on a completely liquid diet, so I made you a calf's liver frappé with onions on the rim of the glass just the way you like it. There you go. Good? Nice and smooth, right? Would you like to see the rest of the house? I've got all the latest do-it-yourself diagnostic equipment so that I can do my own home stress EKGs, myelograms, pelvic sonograms.... I've even rigged the rec room so that on overcast afternoons when I'm feeling especially introspective I can self-administer my own lower GI endoscopies. Oh, do you like that sculpture? I took a sculpture class at the Y and that was my final project. It's called *Father Shaking Flea Powder on His Daughter's Long Greasy Hair with the Indifference of a Sinatra Shaking Grated Parmesan Cheese on a Pile of Linguine*. I was trying to capture that weird kind of indifference, y'know.

—Well, I'm not a critic, I'm an archer—but I think you've definitely captured that sort of very weird... well, I think "indifference" does say it. Oh, by the way, I got new tattoos on my buttocks, would you like to see them?

—Yes, Geoffrey, I'm always interested in seeing anything new that you've done to your buttocks, you know that.

—Well, here they are—what do you think?

—What's that one on the right cheek?

—That's jumper cables entwined around a baguette.

—And what's that one on the left?

—That's the 1040 short form.

—Geoffrey, have you ever given birth to two infants with whiskers and great big bulbous noses like Jimmy Durante and Karl Malden, and every morning you had to shave them before nursing them? Have you, Geoffrey? Have you? Have you...

Tasner stared out the window. From telephone pole to telephone pole, pendulous drops of rainwater dangled from the wires like ornamental money. The meadow was filled with police. Each cop's vaporous breath hovered about his head—a foul nimbus—a nauseating blend of mint mouthwash and rancid coffee—the corners of his mouth glued together with hardened egg yolk. Bored, horny, hung over, underpaid, undereducated, hypoglycemic, the cops ambled through the meadow knocking daffodils off their stems in a black blur of nightsticks.

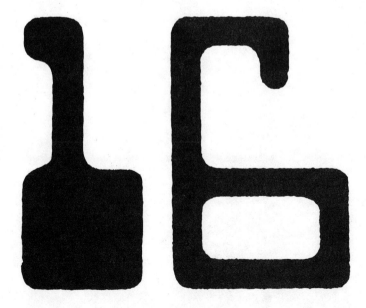

arriet Seibel had the largest, heaviest frontal lobe in Pocahontas High School in Mahwah.

Why does she have the biggest frontal lobe in town? I asked, raising my hand one day in biology class. And no sooner had I asked the innocent question than I was whisked off to the principal's office. All the Pocahontas High VIP's were there: principal, vice-principal, security chief, head of the neurobiology department, faculty advisor to the Eugenics Club, a representative from DARPA (the Defense Advanced Research Projects Agency), and Pocahontas High's media liaison, Mr. Chenowirth.

Don't worry, said the principal, you're not being punished—you just asked a very sensitive question.

Well, why *does* Harriet Seibel have the biggest, heaviest frontal lobe in school? I reinquired.

Maybe I can explain, said Dr. Kline who, with his sharply cut suits and iridescent violet ties and his passion for ballroom dancing and tropical fish, was a perennial favorite of students in and out of neurobiology. You see, he said, Harriet's brain grows heavier because it's developing more synapses.

Well, how can you tell? I asked.

We can tell, Dr. Kline said, because each week when we do a CAT scan and a microscopic examination of her brain tissue we detect pronounced increases in dendrites.... Do you know what dendrites are?

Gosh, Dr. Kline, I said, I don't think we've done that chapter yet.

Dendrites are the filamentous branches of a nerve cell that harvest information from the synapses and forward them to the main body of a cell.

I scribbled notes as quickly as I could and then I looked up. I think she's sad, I said, because the shadow of her head obscures whatever it is she's looking at.

Son, do you know why she's kept in a cage here at Pocahontas over the weekend and fed tapioca pudding the whole time? asked Mr. Chenowirth.

No, I said.

Well, you see, said Dr. Kline, there are more and more toxic pollutants in the atmosphere like chlorine and acrylonitrite, and hydrogen chloride—and the earth's population is increasingly vulnerable to these poisons because it's become too inbred.... The level of genetic homogeneity is so high that our immune systems have been left with too limited a repertoire to defend against the toxic pollutants—so in order for the human species to adapt and survive and prosper we need a dramatic increase in genetic variety—and that requires profoundly exogamous cross-fertilization.

You mean mating with extraterrestrials...with aliens... with spacemen?

Exactly! said everyone, nodding.

And, said Dr. Kline, who would a spaceman from an advanced civilization want to mate with more than the girl with the biggest, heaviest frontal lobe in Pocahontas High School... namely...

Harriet Seibel? I ventured.

Exactly!!

It will be seventeen years ago this winter that I was taken
to the principal's office and first told of Harriet Seibel's strange
plight. Today she lives in Texas—in the Houston Astrodome—
it's the only skull-like structure in the United States that's large
enough to accommodate her brain, which has grown by now to
truly enormous proportions. And as you've probably surmised,
I've fallen in love with Harriet. Being with her is not always
easy and our relationship is a stormy one—after all, she's been
literally fucked all her life by spacemen—and her attitude
toward men is understandably ambivalent but I do love her
very much and we're working on things—a therapist visits us at
the Astrodome once a week for couples counseling . . . so we'll see
what happens.

One last thought—since I've already succumbed to my
nostalgia about those days at Pocahontas High . . . I was
probably the only guy in town who had his own mother as his
high school English teacher. But I'll never figure out the way
she signed my yearbook:

We are merely goose pimples on the arm of the law.

lines composed after

inhaling paint thinner

i like the people, i like the climate, i like the food
marsha was telling me all the bands she liked
i glanced out the window of the computer-run monorail at
the pink hollyhocks and white queen anne's lace and bright
purple wildflowers blooming on the hills and then i looked back
at marsha who was wearing a cream satin two-piece dress, gold
lamé sandals with chain straps, and pearl-drop earrings   she
reeked of cheap perfume   i like cheap perfume on a blond
robot

oh! they're fantastic live! she said   i almost got a
backstage pass to their concert at madison square garden
because i knew this guy who was the hammered dulcimer player
for semen-stained panties and the loose unidentified pubic hairs
and he knew the drummer for cheap perfume on a blond robot,
but this guy had all kinds of physical problems—he was half-
human, half-mole, and part cyborg, i guess, because he had a
nylon fiber-point penis and long-wearing tungsten carbide
testicles and he had to get fetal lamb cell injections and take a

muriatic acid sitz bath every day or the mole half would
overtake the human half and the treatments made him really
moody and capricious—so the day he was supposed to get the
backstage pass to the concert he called up and said, y'know that
broadway show with the TV commercial that goes "can a
proscuitto and provolone sandwich with lettuce and tomatoes
and onions and oil and vinegar irrevocably alter the course of a
man's life—this is the question posed and pondered with
lambent wit and verve in neil simon's delightful new musical,
intrauterine memories of mama"? yeah, i said well, i got
you a ticket for that instead of a backstage pass for the cheap
perfume on a blond robot concert why'd you get me a ticket
for *intrauterine memories of mama* when you knew how much i
wanted to go to the concert, i asked and he said, well, i
guess the fetal lamb cell injections and muriatic acid sitz baths
made me too moody and capricious and i did the wrong thing—
i'm really sorry, marsha and i was pissed but i felt really
bad for him, i mean here was a guy who when he was three
years old played the hammered dulcimer with the astonishing
precosity of a mozart and now look at him his band gets its
first gig in months playing an assembly at an elementary school
and they're supposed to do "home on the range" and he's
supposed to sing, "give me a home where the buffalo roam" and
he stands up there and in all apparent earnestness sings, "give
me a home where the dwarf surf clam and the solitary sea-squirt
roam" and it was pathetic—all the kids were giggling and
shouting, "it's not 'where the dwarf surf clam and the solitary
sea-squirt roam' it's 'where the buffalo roam'!"

i glanced out the window of the computer-run monorail at
the crocodile-infested rivers and malarial swamps teeming with
electric eels and fifteen-foot anacondas and then i looked back at
marsha who was wearing a blush-pink silk blazer over
houndstooth check wool bermuda shorts beneath her synthetic
skin (a latex-like water emulsion polymer the color of café au
lait), a network of white plastic arteries circulated compressed
air throughout her metal and carbon-fiber chassis she

literally had the words hitachi electronics corporation written
all over her   i estimated her development costs to have been
approximately 2 billion yen   she reached behind her head as
if to smooth her hair and inserted a fresh floppy disk into a disk
drive situated inconspicuously at the nape of her
neck   instinctively i reached across to help her and my
fingers brushed against the floppy disk as it receded into the back
of her head   i looked into her sensitive almost vulnerable
pale-blue electron diffraction optical imaging scanners   your
software is so soft, i said   she smiled bashfully, averting her
eyes, and continued to talk about the dulcimer player who was
half-human, half-mole
      shortly after the humiliating fiasco at the elementary
school, i was awakened in the middle of the night by a telephone
call informing me that he had drowned himself in a
fermentation vat at a puerto rican rum distillery   i was told
by a bacardi attorney that he'd flung himself into the vat with a
kind of sublime grace   that his back was arched, his legs
extended, his hands pressed together above his head as if in
prayer   i was told that had it been a competitive dive with
the high and low marks discarded his score would have been
quite impressive   i was told that as he hit the surface of the
fermenting molasses he whispered my name   distraught,
guilt-ridden, confused—i began to see a travel therapist and
after a number of tearful cathartic sessions, she suggested that i
go to europe   i took an apartment upstairs from the cern
atom smasher in switzerland . . . but it was like living over a
bowling alley . . . all that smashing   so i moved back, to a
basement apartment next door to the norad strategic warning
center in colorado under cheyenne mountain   and here i
enjoyed a long overdue respite from the pierced nipple and
enema crowd, here amid the murmuring mountain streams and
craggy cliffs my soul was succored in days of arcadian serenity
and tranquil restoration—often i'd awaken from an afternoon
nap to find a caribou or elk performing a delicate pas de
bourrée on pointed hoof from flagstone to flagstone, his hairy

beer belly spilling over his leotard as he minced about the
carp ponds and pepsi machines that skirted the grounds of
the barbara mandrell in vitro fertilization clinic   i had
a wonderful next-door neighbor—a warmhearted, jovial,
gregarious woman with an irrepressible zest for life   she had
a deep consuming passion for macaroni and cheese and often i'd
awaken from an afternoon nap to find men in white overalls
running a thick black hose from their gleaming cylindrical tank
truck to an inlet valve in the backyard and pumping gallons
and gallons of creamy yellow velveeta cheese sauce into her
underground storage reservoir   one day she said, dear dear
relatives are coming down to visit me from their home in putrid
beef, wyoming   and she ground the wheat and made
pastries   she went hunting in the forest and shot the animals
and ground their flesh into chopped meat for hamburgers   and
she took a boat into the ocean to catch the fish and baked a cake
and threw the fish in for a fish cake   and i asked if i could do
anything to help and she said, no no no, you just go into the
den and watch TV   so i watched a documentary about
norwegian explorer and writer thor heyerdahl proving that it
was possible for a race of primitive people to have migrated
from continent to continent on styrofoam kickboards and i
watched a news conference at which the president announced
that after having reviewed the film *the dirty dozen* with the
trilateral commission he was sending jean harris, claus von
bülow, john delorean, and nine other upper-crust felons to
the caribbean in an armored yawl with a 155-millimeter
champagne bottle mounted on deck capable of firing a 600-lb.
cork from the coastal waters of eastern nicaragua right into
the living room of comandante daniel ortega   a gaunt
pockmarked dissipated handsome sexy mosquito hovered at the
screen window   transfixed as if spaced out on smack   a
thousand images of the flickering sony trinitron reflected in
his compound eyes   his sharp proboscis flashed in the
moonlight like a hypodermic needle with a drop of blood at its
tip   i could tell he was wearing black mesh panties under his

skintight slacks   he undulated his tight little muscular
cylindrical abdomen   it twitched   it shuddered in almost
imperceptible spasms   he was saying, "let me in, marsha" and
"marsha, do you have any sweet shit in your liquor cabinet like
sambuca or kahlúa or peppermint schnapps or amaretto" and
"marsha, don't you recognize me—this is jesus, they freeze-dried
my brain at san quentin" and "marsha, this is elvis...this is
prince"   so i ran and got a can of extra-strength raid and
sprayed him through the screen window until death was his
final reward   the phone was ringing in my apartment   it
rang 50 times   60 times   70 times   80, 90, 100, 110
times   finally on the 117th ring i picked it up...breathless...
panting...it was my cousin, the gastroenterologist   he said,
marsha, you'd better catch the next flight to new york city—your
father's got kidney stones   i flew in and took a taxi right to
mount sinai hospital   when i arrived my father was in the
operating room immersed shoulder-deep in a special high-
tech bathtub   there was a large marshall amplifier next
to the tub   the surgeon turned to the nurse and said,
"guitar"   the nurse handed him a fender stratocaster   the
surgeon strapped it over his shoulder   "guitar pick," he
said   she complied, placing a guitar pick firmly in his gloved
hand   as the surgeon began to play jimi hendrix's solo from
"purple haze," he held the guitar up against the amplifier,
producing howling high-pitched feedback   as my cousin, the
gastroenterologist, later explained, the guitar feedback produces
shock waves in the warm bathwater which travel harmlessly
through the body but shatter the brittle kidney stones into fine
fragments   he said that the guitar-feedback method of
smashing kidney stones had been developed at the monterey pop
institute of kidney, bladder, and urethra disease and had just
been approved by the FDA   i trusted my cousin's medical
explication as i trusted my cousin—implicitly   esteemed
by his professional colleagues, affluent, and socially prominent,
he was the shining scion of his immigrant family—although
his father had achieved considerable notoriety in his own

vocation—baseball   he'd been the first rigidly orthodox
soviet-style marxist-leninist to pitch for a major league
team   this was thanks to the enlightened and farsighted
hiring practices of brooklyn dodgers owner branch rickey who
signed my uncle in the early 50s, to the almost unanimous
displeasure of organized baseball   my uncle caused
tremendous controversy when he refused to pitch on may
day and later declined the opening start of a world series
because it fell on the wedding anniversary of ethel and julius
rosenberg   notwithstanding one's political affiliations one
couldn't deny his baseball prowess, and in fact he had such an
incredible spitball that his salivary glands were insured by
lloyd's of london   we were reminiscing over falafel
sandwiches and diet cokes in the mount sinai cafeteria when my
cousin's face took on an unexpectedly somber aspect   what's
wrong, i asked, do you have food allergies?   is the wheat
gluten in the pita bread causing you to become moody and
capricious?   is the nutrasweet in the diet coke making you
epileptic?   no, he said, it's your father...there's more wrong
with him than just the kidney stones   we discovered a gas
pocket of freon in his brain   what's freon? i asked   freon's
a refrigerant used in air-conditioning systems   and he looked
at me and with the grim urgency of a network anchorman he
said, marsha, the freon bubble in your father's brain is the work
of terrorists   your father was #1 on the trilateral
commission's hit parade   well, can't you just install a
replacement head? i asked   every body comes with two or
three replacement heads and instructions on removing the
worn-out head and installing the spare   to remove your
head simply take your left hand and hold the back of your
head   take your right hand and hold your chin firmly in its
palm   twist your head sharply with a counterclockwise
motion until you hear it disengage   to install your
replacement head place the head assembly on neck housing and
insert guide pins through mounting holes   hold head firmly
in position with both hands and rotate slowly clockwise until

assembly locks into place   if your replacement head features
a built-in dish antenna you can test head function by standing
in the middle of your backyard and determining whether you're
picking up any satellite signals   if your replacement head
fails to pick up any satellite signals then you either installed
your head improperly or the head is defective   if, after
installing new head, you are unable to discern the contradictions
in capitalist modes of production, you have either installed
your head improperly or head is defective
     i glanced out the window of the computer-run monorail at
the feed store, the international harvester dealership, the
barbershop, the county courthouse, and the domed tabernacle
of the aryan nazarene church and then i looked back at
marsha   at the epicanthic folds of her japanese-made eyes,
at her olive silk pleated tunic and smoke-blue wool crepe
pants   and in the periphery of my vision i noticed a group
of caucasian hoodlums entering the car   i think they were
delinquents from one of the bad parts of canada   recalling
the fashion of urban black youth of the 1970s who wore combs
and afro picks in their hair, these caucasian thugs took it one
step further—they wore *all* their grooming implements and
toilet articles   they swaggered down the aisle with q-tips
sticking out of their ears, strands of dental floss hanging from
their teeth, and big globs of styling mousse on the tops of their
heads   they were apparently a gang of deaf caucasian punks
because instead of toting boom boxes on their shoulders, they
each carried a letter-quality printer which churned out the
lyrics of the songs   they began to terrorize the women and
elderly passengers   i rose in my seat and stepped into the
aisle you're dead meat, i said, slowly enough so that they could
read my lips   i'm the last of the great musclemen   for
100 years musclemen ruled the u.s.a.   a muscleman sat in
the oval office, coconut butter slathered across his bursting
rippling physique   the senate and house of representatives
and supreme court were filled with musclemen and
musclewomen   the mayor of new york city was an

immense musclewoman—165 lbs. of steroid-scented beefcake
garnished with a red bikini that marked her bulging latitudes
like two rubber bands about to snap   but then the
engineers with their microchips and modems overcame the
musclepeople   well, i'm the last of the great iron-pumping
vigilantes   i cornered each one of those q-tip–sporting
caucasian animals and beat him with my huge fists until his
face was a pudding of flesh and blood and his lower lip
protruded stupidly from his mouth like the heavy petal of a
summer flower

after freshening up in the monorail lavatory, i retired to
the dining car for a bit of supper   what color is your
mozzarella? i asked the waitress   it's pink—it's the same color
as the top of a mennen lady speed stick antiperspirant
dispenser, y'know that color?   no, ma'am, i said   it's the
same pink they use for the gillette daisy disposable razors for
women ... y'know that color?   nope   y'know the pink they
use on the wrappers for carefree panty shields?   nuh-
uh   well, it's the same pink as pepto-bismol, y'know that
color?   oh yeah, i said, well, do you have spaghetti?   well,
what's spaghetti?   it's elongated thin solid strings of pasta
no, we don't have that, but i want to tell you, mister, that no
matter what you order tonight you're in for a treat because
our new chef was a texas death row chef   what's that? i
asked   well, the state of texas is executing so many convicts
that it's been forced to hire special death row chefs to
accommodate the spiraling number of last meal requests—a
condemned inmate being of course traditionally entitled to
the final menu of his choice   in the old days, when capital
punishment was infrequent enough to be noteworthy and when
death sentences were meted out primarily to the itinerant and
impecunious, steaks or cheeseburgers with a side of french fries
or onion rings, coffee, and pie à la mode tended to be the order
of the day   but today, murder, mayhem, random violence,
heinous brutality, and wanton slaughter of innocent life is just
as likely to occur in corporate boardrooms, health spas, tanning

salons, and video clubs as it is in slum alleyways and backwoods motels   this coupled with your gastronomic education in the public schools and wardens are finding themselves obliged to accommodate last requests for everything from *coquilles st. jacques* and roast pheasant with chestnut stuffing to braised veal shanks, milan style, and cold sautéed trout in orange marinade   electric chairs, gas chambers, and firing squads are working at such a frenetic pace that death row kitchens are sites of frantic raucous activity, with depleted items being constantly scrawled on the 86 board and waiters rushing in and out and yelling their orders: i got a steak *au poivre,* a stuffed sole, an order of fried zucchini sticks and cancel the bay scallops—governor's pardon . . . the kitchen lights intermittently dimming as power surges to the electric chair   ads for death row chefs and death row sauciers appear in all the major trade publications and the cornell school of hotel/motel management and the new jersey culinary institute offer degrees in last meal preparation   students are trained in every aspect and nuance of death row cuisine including which wines more felicitously complement meals preceding death by firing squad and which wines more felicitously complement meals preceding death by lethal injection   sounds good, i said, let me try that roast pheasant with chestnut stuffing   we don't have that   how about the cold sautéed trout in orange marinade, that sounded good   nope, we don't have that   what about those braised veal shanks?   nuh-uh   then why don't you give me a cheeseburger with a side of french fries, coffee, and pie à la mode   thanks for your order, mister   i took a long drink of ice water   my bruised raw fists ached from the beating i'd administered to those thugs   i slumped down into the vinyl-upholstered banquette   my body was exhausted   my head felt like a buoy, bobbing on the surface of the water   i tried to forget my own exhaustion, my own pain, by eavesdropping on the conversation of a man and a woman in the adjoining booth and i concentrated with such focused intensity that during lulls in their conversation i could hear the secretions

of their internal glands drip with the audibility of leaking
faucets   they were both happily married to their respective
spouses, but they desperately wanted to have a love affair with
each other   unwilling to risk jeopardizing their marriages,
they'd decided that on a preordained night they would meet
in each other's dreams and that way they could consummate
their passion for each other without actually, statutorily
transgressing their conjugal vows   they would make a
kind of oneiric tryst   they would have a sort of out-of-body
affair   they'd agreed that the day after this prearranged
night they would meet in the dining car of the computer-run
monorail to compare the delights of their telepathic liaison
i don't think they'd been there long when i started listening
where were you last night? the man said angrily   what are
you talking about? asked the woman   well, all i dreamt of
last night was sitting on the bank of a stream eating a turkey
salad platter garnished with mandarin oranges   that was me!
exclaimed the woman   what? said the man   i *was* the
mandarin oranges or i should say i appeared in your dream in
the form of mandarin oranges—because they are sweet and
tart and small and cool like me—i was symbolized in your
dream by mandarin oranges   well, this is very annoying, said
the man, why couldn't you have simply appeared in my dream
as you, like we planned?   well...thought the woman, and
then after a prolonged pause she said, well, you have some nerve
being annoyed—where were you last night?   the man
squirmed a bit in his seat   why, he asked, what did you
dream?   i dreamt i was lying on a beach blanket on an
endless asphalt field in indiana, thoroughly basted with suntan
lotion, reading lee iacocca's autobiography and a squadron of
french mirage-2000 jet fighters kept flying back and forth above
the field in tight wing formation   the man averted his eyes
sheepishly, that was me, he said, i appeared in your dream in
the form of mirage-2000 jets...but i didn't mean to! i intended
to come as myself   well, said the woman indignantly, i
certainly didn't mean to appear in your dream as mandarin
oranges—i had every intention of appearing in your dream in

the flesh!   the man reached across the table and took the
woman's hand in his   i wish you had, he said softly   this
is the problem, said the woman, although we intend to appear
as ourselves—we are apparently transmogrified en route
into each other's dreams into encoded images or symbols of
ourselves   this is quite unsatisfying, said the man, how will
we ever recognize each other?   we'll simply have to assume
that any elements congruent with those which appeared last
night represent each other   you're right, said the man, now i
know that any time i encounter a garnish in my dreams it's
you—every olive, every tomato slice, candied apple, parsley
sprig, lemon rind, grated radish, and maraschino cherry—it's
you!   yes, said the woman, and i know that each time i
discover an F-16 or a MIG-25 or a strategic air command
bomber or a 747 passenger plane or the space shuttle or even a
soviet SAM-7 surface-to-air missile—it's you...you and only
you!
    i found the lovers' passionate predicament and their
passionately ingenious solution quite poignant   not only was
i moved by the sophistication of their microcomponents—only
fourth-generation robots were capable of dreaming and
telepathy—but they made me think back to the springtime of
my own youth, when i first fell in love   the year was
1958   cary grant and sophia loren starred in a motion
picture called *houseboat*   it was a beautifully tender love
story of an italian conductor's daughter and a widowed father
of three small children   to me it was the most romantic film
of my lifetime   and i thought that sophia loren was the
most potent embodiment of erotic love imaginable   i suffered
the agonies of an enraptured adolescent   i can remember
vividly the very sweetness of my longing, the hot sudorific
intensity of fantasies inevitably doused in the icy realization of
my desire's futility...absently doodling her name on my gym
shorts   "sophia"..."sophia"...the word reverently multiplied
on every wall of the weight room, scratched even in the vinyl-
covered benches of my nautilus equipment   she was the first
and last woman i ever loved   although cary grant and sophia

loren appeared larger than life on screen, they were actually 10-inch scale models—graphite-reinforced shells of polycarbonate polybutylene resin filled with cellular urethane foam—designed and constructed by special-effect artists at toho films, the japanese studio also responsible for godzilla, rodan, mothra, and ghidrah

after finishing my cheeseburger, coffee, and dessert, i paid my check and repaired to the bar car for a brandy   i had just settled onto my bar stool when i felt the firm grip of a biometal hand on my shoulder   i swiveled around and for a second was so nonplussed that i didn't recognize the sallow and sunken-cheeked figure before me   it was a painter i'd known quite some time ago when i lived on reade street   featuring a gyroscopic balance sensor, enhanced manual dexterity, advanced irony and image appropriation functions, and a 600K-byte art history memory, he was the first of the automaton painters to exhibit simultaneously at boone, castelli, and radio shack, and to appear in the same month on the covers of *art forum* and *popular mechanics*   and he was the first automaton painter equipped with a functional gastrointestinal tract enabling him to eat at mr. chow's   he appeared to me to be in a state of extreme agitation and although we hadn't seen each other in some twenty years, he forwent any pleasantries and steered me roughly from the bar   come with me to my loft car, he said, i want you to see my new painting—i think it's the best work i've ever done   every computer-run monorail had five or six loft cars—usually towards the back of the train   these loft cars were reserved for artists to enable them to work on their paintings or sculptures without interruption between stations   so with me in tow, he proceeded hurriedly to his loft car   the painting was propped against the side of the car, draped in a section of tarpaulin   let me give you some background before you see it, he said   two men get out of prison after 10-year stretches for armed robbery   in a shared fit of spontaneous recidivism, they immediately steal a bright red mustang convertible   they're driving along and they approach a huge billboard depicting a voluptuous woman in a

very scanty, revealing bikini   the men, neither of whom has
seen or been with a real woman in 10 years, are overcome with
desire   they slam on the brakes—the red mustang swerves
and screeches to a halt in a roadside ditch   and the two
men get out of the car, rip their clothes off, throw themselves
across the hot hood of the mustang, and begin to furiously
masturbate   and the red mustang is so hot from the engine
and the desert sun that when they ejaculate the globs of semen
literally fry on the hood   and that's the painting, he said,
releasing the tarpaulin   and so it was—there was the desert
road, the lean muscular etiolated bodies of the two ex-cons
sprawled exhaustedly across a red mustang convertible, two
large albuminous pools of fresh semen sizzling on its hot hood
like two fried eggs   this is a numinous work of art if i ever
painted one, he said, this painting is extremely spooky   it's
like the portrait of dorian gray or something   it frightens
the living shit out of me   what is it that frightens you about
it? i asked   the painting is protean...it's unstable...it
changes!   what do you mean? i asked   i mean the painting
literally changes depending on where the monorail is—the
painting transforms itself—it apparently metamorphoses its
pigments to reflect the location of the monorail—it's like some
kind of weird window!   well, it didn't take me more than
a couple of seconds to realize that it *was* a window   and
if there had been any doubts, they were dispelled as the
monorail began to pull away and, through the window, the red
convertible and the two pale and spent convicts receded in the
distance and the setting desert sun cast a coral light on the
landscape

     i walked away, deeply moved by the refusal or inability
of this robot to distinguish between the factitious and the
natural   but a powerful turbulent hungry feeling was welling
up within me   i longed for the warm textures of flesh and
blood—the faint glimmers of sympathy and pleasure in a
pair of eyes indicating the presence of a heart and nerves
and synapses and not gallium arsenide chips and integrated
circuits   perhaps i'm the last human being on earth with an

abiding system of ethics and a beautiful body   although on
certain beaches beautiful heavily muscled proletarian boys are
cracking open horseshoe crabs with ball-peen hammers and
sucking out their 175-million-year-old deoxyribonucleic acid in
a gallant effort to rejuvenate the human species   but i am
nostalgic for more romantic times   i slipped into a camisole
top of silver and violet mesh, a black velvet skirt, a sapphire
and opal necklace, diamond earrings, and a pair of multicolored
python pumps   and i made my way, car by car, through
the computer-run monorail—cruising for sentient beings

about the author

I was born on January 4, 1956, at
Margaret Hague Hospital in Jersey
City, New Jersey. Little is known about my early life. My
father, Joel, and my mother, Muriel, kept me with them in
Jersey City. Often they would take me to look at dinosaur bones
at the Museum of Natural History, and then, invariably, I
would be given ravioli. Summers were spent at the Jersey shore
in a town called Deal which is near Long Branch where Ulysses
Grant spent his presidential summers. It should also be noted
that from the stoop of our little house in Jersey City I could
discern the screen at the Newark Drive-In Movie Theatre. When
I was six, my sister Debbie was born. (An actress and former
shoe model, she has since changed her name to "Chase.") One
day we moved to West Orange, where I saw my first squirrel.
On my first day at school in West Orange I was asked to do
something that I refused to do: skip. When I saw the Beatles on
television in 1963, I decided that I'd like to be an "artist." At
various times the Leyner family went to Holland, England,
Denmark, Sweden, and Portugal. In junior high school,

there were only three girls shorter than I was—two were identical twins and one was Shelly Ullman, whom I asked to wear my ID bracelet. Unfortunately her wrist was too pudgy to accommodate the bracelet without her hand becoming gangrenous. Bringing great honor to my people, I was chosen as one of the starting pitchers in the Little League All-Star Game. I began writing poetry. I attended Columbia High School, where I wrote a column called "This Side of Paradise" for the school paper. The column chronicled the parties that my friends and I attended. In high school, I loved to rock 'n' roll, a hot dog made me lose control. I was in a band that broke up over artistic differences—I wanted us to go "glitter," à la T. Rex, Bowie, the New York Dolls; the other guitarist, Tom Cacherelli, wanted us to be a more workmanlike band like the Allman Brothers. I graduated from high school when I was sixteen and dashed off to the Middle East with my girlfriend Liz Ross, who today is a lawyer in Boston. Eventually, sick of falafel, we dashed off to Greece, Switzerland, and France before returning to the U.S.A. to attend our respective universities: Radcliffe for Liz and Brandeis for me. In 1972 my poem about Tina Turner appeared in *Rolling Stone*—my career was launched! Then I met Sarah "Calamity Jane" Vogelman and offered her a quaalude, and so began our college romance—today Sarah is married to Adam Kariotakis and has two kids; she's a lawyer in New Brunswick. I began writing fiction at Brandeis, and when I graduated in 1977, I was awarded the Dorothy Moyer Memorial Award for writing. I was offered fellowships at the graduate writing programs at Johns Hopkins University and at the University of Colorado in Boulder. I went to Boulder, got my M.A. in 1979, and then moved to Washington, D.C., where "Calamity Jane" Vogelman was living and I had a series of stupid jobs and began work on *I Smell Esther Williams*. I moved to Hoboken in 1982 and worked as an advertising copywriter for Panasonic for a year. I dated a bass player named Trude Koby, who was also going out with Fab Five Freddy at the time—today she's a lawyer in Miami. In 1983, *I Smell Esther Williams* was published by the Fiction Collective.

That year I met Arleen Portada, and in 1984 I asked her to marry me. She got very embarrassed and ran into the bathroom; eventually she came out and said "yes" and we were married and had a riotous party at—where else?—the Hoboken Elks' Club. Arleen is a brilliant psychotherapist. She was asked to appear on "The Morton Downey Show" and refused. We've traveled to places all over the country including Fayetteville, North Carolina. My work began appearing in various magazines. In 1986, I was awarded a fellowship grant from the New Jersey State Council on the Arts. I've given readings at many distinguished venues, including the New York City Department of Cultural Affairs, the West Side Y's Writer's Voice series, Columbia University, Illinois State University, SUNY Buffalo etc. While working on *My Cousin, My Gastroenterologist,* I supported myself by doing advertising copywriting. Recently I've written ads for biodegradable incontinence briefs and artificial saliva. No one knows what the future holds in store for me.